KARMA NATION

Mohan Ashtakala

Copyrights

Dedication and Acknowledgements

This book is dedicated to my spiritual teacher Dr. T.D. Singh (Bhaktisvarupa Damodara Swami.) He lives forever in his follower's hearts.

This novel was possible only through the contributions of many people. My many thanks to the Tiwa community of Taos Pueblo in Taos, New Mexico; the Pastor and Deacons of the Antioch Missionary Baptist Church in Houston, Texas; Priestess Miriam of the Voodoo Spiritual Temple in New Orleans, Louisiana; the Louisiana Civil War Museum, in New Orleans; Jeanine Jones of Stone Mountain Park, Atlanta, Georgia and the staff of the Old Slave Mart Museum in Charleston, South Carolina.

My special thanks to Reverend John Thompson of Columbia, South Carolina, Panchali devi Walford, Anne Marie Emerson McDonald, Pranada Comptois, Cassie Welburn and Robin van Eck for their comments and suggestions.

The fifteenth chapter of Karma Nation is dedicated to Ralph Ellison, author of Juneteenth (Random House, 1999.)

Finally, I had the great privilege of traveling through the American South with my son, Rishi, and visiting the places mentioned in this novel. A road trip for the ages, with one of my favorite people. May we share further adventures!

Permission

The author acknowledges permission received from Dr. Charles A. Taylor for the use of material from his book Juneteenth: A Celebration of Freedom, published by Open Hand Publishing, 2002

Chapter One

Boulder, Colorado, was not the hippie hangout Chantley's mother had described in her letters. True, occasional headshops graced its streets, street buskers strummed their guitars, and Nepali import stores sold colorful Indian cotton skirts much like the one she wore, but the college town had become gentrified. Chantley shook her head. Her wanderings over the last few days revealed the real students crowded the pizza joints and cheap bars on the Hill, letting the downtown pedestrian-only Mall live off its worn-out reputation as a center of anti-establishmentarian hippiedom of the sixties. She glanced around the street running right down Boulder's center. Fortunately, with gentrification came amenities: flower beds of red carnations and yellow gladioli, wooden benches and maple trees to provide shade.

Chantley checked her address book again. Nothing made sense. Did the very buildings move or disappear? Everything looked new: fancy, architecturally-designed structures built of brick, glass and natural materials, beautifully constructed and obviously expensive, yet discreet and unostentatious.

The summer heat escaped from the cement sidewalks and floated past the display windows of trendy boutiques exhibiting preppy dresses few students could afford. It billowed above Starbucks selling ten-dollar lattes and disappeared into the sky over terraced restaurants serving expensive glasses of wine to out-of-towners.

Chantley wiped her brow with her hand, though the heat didn't bother her. In the hills above Mysuru, India, where she grew up, the temperature felt comparable. No, it was the stress which got to her. In the five days since her arrival, nothing had gone right. How long would it take to find her mother? And did she still live here?

Did Chantley make a mistake in leaving India? Despite being a white American woman, she felt thoroughly Indian, having spent her entire life there. Here, in the country of her ancestors, everything felt alien. America confounded Chantley. She felt strange approaching Americans, worried her accent would give her away as a naïve foreigner.

Vijay. I wouldn't be here if not for Vijay. The bruise on her heart still hurt. She pursed her lips and sighed. After it ended, she understood she had no future in India. I need to move on. I have to gain courage.

It proved difficult to get anyone to stop, let alone sit and have a conversation, and she believed it impossible to navigate all this strangeness by herself. What a difference from ashram life in India, where someone familiar, where help, always existed! She suddenly stopped. What made her think she could find her mother? That they would reconnect after sixteen years?

Chantley looked up into the cloudless Colorado sky, breathed deeply, and struggled to quell the panic in her heart. Gulping, she pushed back the tears threatening to erupt. She pulled her long brown hair behind her ears, steeled her green eyes and looked ahead. A few parents sat talking to each other, their children playing near the fountains, as street musicians strummed their guitars and everyone else dashed back and forth. She spied a young man sitting on a bench five feet away, insulated in a shell of silence, his legs stretched out, crossed at the ankles, head buried in a book, the sun reflecting on his black skin. She glanced at the title: Black Skin, White Masks, and briefly wondered what that meant.

She walked up. "Excuse me..."

The man didn't move.

"Excuse me," she repeated, this time tapping him on the shoulder.

Looking up, the man pushed his glasses up his nose. When he gazed into her eyes, a current of intense attraction surged through her every nerve and muscle. She instantly turned away. The world moved in slow motion, yet she reeled. The scent of the flowers, previously so subtle as to be almost unnoticeable, overpowered her with their pungent sweetness. Her face turned red and hot. My God, she thought, what's happening to me? I've never felt anything like this before!

She turned around and peered at him again, hardly noticing his features, frozen by his intense brown eyes. He dropped the book on the bench and jumped up, mouth open, hands stretched out, with surprise, even shock, showing on his face.

"Are you okay?" he asked.

Chantley stopped. Did a fleeting sense of déjà-vu appear in his eyes? A powerful experience of having previously met arose, maybe from another life, perhaps in another place. She remembered Guru-ji's statement at the ashram: there is a reason for everyone we meet. That strong reactions upon encountering someone for the first time give the clearest indications of a karmic past. Their eyes met again; his widened, and hers narrowed. She stood staring awkwardly.

"What is it?" he asked.

"I don't know if this makes any sense, but I have a feeling that I know you." *Oh my God, what am I doing,* she thought. *Did I just say that?*

He jerked his head back. "What do you mean?"

She hesitated. "Maybe we share a karmic past," she offered, her eyes unfocused, her head shaking in confusion.

The man's laughed. "Don't I know you from a previous life?" he said, mimicking her soft, clipped accent. "That's a great pick-up line. I'm going to have to remember that!"

Chantley turned red. "I'm sorry," she mumbled. In India, people understood karmic attachments. He might think it strange, but the recognition crossing his eyes was undeniable. She decided to say nothing. Taking a deep breath, she slowed her racing heart and collected her wits. *Thank God for the meditation lessons at the ashram!* Calming herself, she slid into relaxation. If a connection existed, it would reveal itself naturally without pressing the issue.

He quickly gathered himself. "No. No, that's okay. You kind of surprised me." He held out his hand and smiled. "I'm Sam."

Sam wore a clean white shirt, brown slacks and glasses with strong black frames while a bowler hat sat cocked on his head. When he smiled, creases formed at the corners of his eyes and the edges of his mouth. As his large warm hands enveloped hers, her heart jumped again. His presence felt hyper-real, as if accidentally encountering a famous actor from a classic film.

"You look like one of those hippie students who hang around Boulder," he remarked.

Chantley examined her white, short-sleeved, Indian-cotton blouse with stitched red embroidery, long cream-colored skirt featuring a printed blue paisley design, brown-cloth shoulder bag dangling from her right shoulder and flat runners on her feet.

"But you're not from around here, are you?"

"No, I'm from India."

"Yes," remarked Sam. "I kind of recognized that accent." He pushed his glasses up his nose again. "But you look American."

Chantley nodded. "My parents are American, but I grew up in India."

"And you speak English real well."

Real well? She stroked her chin, pondering his phrasing. "Oh, you mean 'very well.'"

Sam laughed. "You speak the language better than me."

She was about to correct his grammar but caught herself. "I studied at an English language school in India," she said. "They're quite common."

"What are you doing here?"

"I'm searching for my mother. It's a long story.'

Sam gave her an expansive smile. He moved to one side of the bench. "Do you want to sit down and tell me?"

Chantley felt both awkward and attracted. The Women's College in Mysuru, where she had studied, offered few opportunities for interaction with men. Having spent all her life around Indians made her feel at ease with this man's dark good looks. She sized him up. He reminded her of a young Rajnikanth, whose movie star good looks and smoldering eyes made her girlfriends squirm.

She accepted the invitation, sat down, and revealed what she could—at least, what she felt comfortable divulging to someone she had just met: that she was born in India; her father lay buried in a grave there, and her mother left her when Chantley was just three. She didn't, couldn't, reveal that hers was a desperate running away from a broken heart. Her hunt for her mother constituted not just an attempt at reconnection but a frantic search for who she was and, in that lost identity, an attempt to discover her future.

She reached into her bag and pulled out a tin box decorated with large painted blue flowers, opened the lid, and pulled out a picture of her mother taken under the eucalyptus trees at the ashram. The photo showed a young woman with light brown hair and a garland of marigolds draped around her neck, smiling in the sun, but with a hint of sadness around her eyes. Their only other connection was a small stack of letters hidden in the same container. Written in childish language, they appeared regularly for a few years, then less often, and stopped entirely when she reached seven. She imagined her mother's chestnut curls turning gray, fancied the appearance of wrinkles on the face, the smile fading over time and the sadness around the eyes being replaced by a growing darkness. After Sam examined it for a few seconds, she pushed the picture back into the box, sealed it and, once again, concealed it in her bag.

She picked up the address book and pointed to a line. "I'm looking for building number 1162. The numbers stop at 1150," she offered. "And the next block starts at 1200."

Sam peered at the book. "I don't recognize that address."

Chantley sighed anxiously. Another dead end. Yet she did not want to get up and leaving. Something about Sam kept her in her seat. "And you?" she asked, changing the subject.

"I'm graduating from University next month."

She eyed him curiously. "What are you studying?"

"American History."

"What's that about?" As soon as she asked the question, she felt foolish. What am I thinking? How can anyone summarize four years of study in a few quick sentences?

"It's all about rocks."

Her eyes opened wide. "What?"

"American history is about rocks."

"Really?"

"When the pilgrims arrived in America, they landed on a rock."

She nodded her head uncertainly.

"When we Americans reached Virginia, we broke through the Appalachians. Then we smashed mountains of coal in Kentucky."

"Okay," she said, forehead knotted, following his statements hesitantly.

"In Michigan, huge excavators mining hills of iron ore. Chain gangs splitting granite in Georgia, miners blasting metal ore in Minnesota, chiselers chiseling marble in Vermont."

Chantley caught on. She smiled.

"Crushed enough gravel to build a million miles of highway, broke enough rock to dam every river in the country, split enough stone to build stupendous skyscrapers. We smashed Santa Fe, fractured Phoenix, cracked California, and shattered San Francisco."

"Is that so?"

"Uh-huh. We leveled the mountains of Montana, pebbled all of Pennsylvania, ruptured rock in Rhode Island."

"That's a lot of rocks!"

"Yes. Enough rocks to fill a million Taj Mahals. More than a thousand Great Walls of China. As many as in a hundred thousand Egyptian pyramids."

"Wow!"

"We rocked the Rockies. Bouldered Boulder. Stoned Stone Mountain."

She giggled.

He stopped and waved his finger at her in all seriousness. "Americans broke rocks as if they knew that, one day, the rocks would break them!"

Chantley burst out laughing. *What the heck did that mean?* "You're funny!" she remarked, admiring his inventiveness, his intelligence.

Sam beamed. "And that is American History." He got up on his feet. "Let's look for your building," he suggested, glancing back and forth.

They roamed up and down the street, checking and rechecking addresses, but the mysterious building couldn't be found. Chantley imagined every gray-haired woman they passed on the streets to be her mother but never got the courage to question any of them. Her one and only attachment to this place—the address, besides the eighteen-year-old picture—proved to be false. When darkness fell, they reluctantly called it quits.

"About fifteen years ago, developers renovated many of these buildings," explained Sam. "Boulder's changed a lot over the years. We can meet tomorrow at the University and check the land records. That may solve the mystery."

Chantley nodded her head.

Chapter Two

Upper Boulder Canyon, where the rich lived in homes the size of small palaces, boasted priceless views of mountains, forests and pristine lakes. Chantley looked up. Like a Bavarian castle, the house occupied the top of a small ridge and blended perfectly with the surroundings with its long, sloping, cedar-shingled roof and gray stone walls.

She wondered why just two people, Candace and Charles, would need so much room. A whole Indian village could fit inside the building. Having grown up in rural India, in small but comfortable quarters, enveloped by the egalitarianism of the ashram and their everyday experiences, she had naively assumed everyone shared similar circumstances. She never imagined any visiting yoga students could be in a class much wealthier than the others. Of course, many students who visited the ashram were less affluent. They had scraped their dollars together for years to attend the classes there. Yet, she felt immense gratitude for Candace's hospitality and for sharing her home. Chantley decided to repay the generosity with the only currency she could afford—free yoga classes. The idea meshed well with her ambitions: to do good in the world.

She opened the large oak doors with her key and entered a foyer the size of her entire living quarters in India. To the right of the vestibule stood an open living room large enough for several sofas, love seats, tables, television sets and a fireplace constructed of local fieldstone. Charles, Candace's boyfriend, lay sprawled on the nearest sofa.

"I'm watching a movie I know you'll like," he said. "Why don't you join me?"

She excused herself. "I'm tired."

She clambered up the blonde oak wood staircase that hugged the wall to her left. The sizeable second-floor area, with floor-to-ceiling glass, drew her to the windows. She paused, gazing at the valley below and the fir trees spread like a dark green carpet. A fleece of fog, wrapped around distant peaks, glowed softly in the moonlight.

She turned right and, after passing several locked doors, came to her room, entered, removed her shoes and lay in her bed. The day indeed differed from the previous ones in America. The first day had been a blur: the landing at Denver International Airport, the long drive from the eastern flatlands, the rush through the industrial and urban areas of the city and the slow ascent into the hills. The jet lag, the blocked ears and the stiff legs from the twenty-six-hour flight from Mysuru, not to mention a five-hour layover at Heathrow, had wiped her out.

Her next day remained a dull haze. She had spent much of the time in bed, adjusting to the new time zone and feeling discombobulated when she did venture out. With its vibrant colors, incessant sounds and an endless variety of people, India assaulted one's senses, whereas everything proved to be so much more muted here. There, a distinct earthy aroma emanated from the land, and she missed waking to the fragrance of firewood the hill-folk burned in the early mornings. The dry air here smelled more astringent, antiseptic and, somehow, less organic. Or, maybe, it was just Colorado with its thin mountain air.

Candace's boyfriend solicitously drove her to Boulder the next few days, even though she protested his unexpected assistance. She had wandered the city, getting the lay of the land and its inhabitants while searching for the address.

But this day proved to be unique. She touched her chest with her fingers. Her heart still raced. Her head still swirled. She breathed deeply, calmed herself, and replayed the day's events. The attraction upon meeting Sam proved undeniable. *Did he feel the same? Didn't he betray a shock of recognition at first sight? Or am I fooling myself?*

How could they share past lives? She shook her head. Fifteen thousand miles separated their birthplaces, not to mention their differing ethnicities. How much different could their experiences be? Yet, what could explain the deliciousness of sentiment felt upon meeting him? *I'd love to see how we're connected.* Her mind wandered. *There's no reason we couldn't have been lovers in a past life.*

She sat up in alarm. *What am I doing? Why am I going there?* When Vijay broke off with her, it was torture, a year-long affliction. *Didn't I promise to never put myself in that situation again?* The intense feelings for Vijay, maybe as strong as what she now felt, raised a disturbing question. Did this define her modus operandi—to become intensely attached to men only to feel disappointment later?

Rubbing her forehead, she reminded herself that time and finances wouldn't allow for distraction. She came to locate her mother and risked everything on the mission. If she failed, a yawning emptiness threatened to swallow her up.

Being only three when her mother left, she had been far too young to have concrete, continuous memories of her. Bits and pieces remained: holding her mother's elegant hands while shopping in Mysuru, being fed a cup of warm milk in the mornings at the ashram and, towards the end, her mother's lonely eyes. Chantley didn't remember her mother leaving, only the puzzlement afterward, of not knowing what happened and, years later, finally understanding that her mother was gone.

An only child, cast off by her father's death and forsaken in love, she now naturally grasped at the last remaining straw: her mother.

She gulped. *Am I chasing a fantasy? Is this a desperate attempt at avoiding reality, a running away from fear?* She lay back, shut her eyelids tight and pushed back the panic. *I can't go down that path. If I do, I'll lose everything.*

Sam offered his help, and naturally, she accepted. *Thank God.* She had no choice. Besides Candace, he constituted the only person who provided assistance. *But I'm not going to allow myself to become attached to Sam. After all, I don't want another Vijay on my hands.*

*****

Sam sat on the edge of his bed in the dorm room he shared with DeAngelo. The strictly utilitarian room contained two beds, a couple of dressers, a desk for each and a window that overlooked the now-dark housing quad. They formed an odd pair. Sam thrived in chaos, whereas DeAngelo liked the place neat and organized. Sam hardly ever dressed up, but DeAngelo specialized in preppy clothes. Sam studied history, whereas his roommate majored in engineering. But despite their apparent differences, DeAngelo proved to be his best friend, whose straight and clear thinking tempered Sam's sometimes wild intellectual ramblings.

Sam gazed out the window. He found Chantley utterly fascinating. Her clothes, good looks, her accent, her story; a genie bursting out of a lamp could not have surprised him more. She was one in a million. He replayed their meeting. The sun had formed a luminous halo over her head and reflected a thousand times on the ends of her long brown strands. He couldn't bear it and had to shield his eyes with his hands. Her face had turned white upon seeing him, her eyes opening wide and unflinching, as if stumbling across a long-lost friend. It had unnerved him, but he couldn't stop staring right back. For a moment, he had lost his breath—never had he felt such an instant attraction to a woman.

He whistled. Why did she look at him like that? When she mentioned karma, he had taken it as a sly attempt to strike up a conversation, but her confusion upon his reply suggested otherwise, as if she really believed it. He shook his head. *What a strange way to look at the world! Maybe it's just her culture.*

Her Indian background aroused his curiosity. His readings on Black History naturally led to an interest in colonization worldwide. He had studied little literature on the topic from Indian writers. He admitted not knowing much of the traditional culture of that country. He rocked his head back and forth. She seemed so untouched by Western ideas.

Another thought struck him. Chantley seemed young. Not in age, since freshmen resembling high-schoolers filled the campus, but in her wide-eyed, Alice-in-Wonderland expression, like a lost soul in a strange new world. He caught himself. Of course, she's lost; she's new to this country. He pursed his lips. *Anyway, everyone looks young to me. At twenty-five, I'm the oldest in my class.*

DeAngelo walked in and placed his briefcase on the chair in front of his desk. Sam knew of no other student who carried a briefcase to class. He smiled at his friend's idiosyncrasy.

"Hey bro, what's up?" asked his friend.

"Just chilling," replied Sam. "Met a girl at the Mall."

"Uh-huh."

"Yeah. Really strange."

"What's that?"

"She's from India, but she's white."

DeAngelo cocked his head. "I got a couple of guys from India in my Fluid Dynamics class. They're brown. You know, like, dark brown."

"She's American, but she grew up in India."

"You like her?"

Sam considered the question. His heart had pounded the instant he saw Chantley, and unusually, he even became tongue-tied. More, he noticed the feelings to be mutual. But at the same time, he detected a millisecond of hesitancy from her, not obvious but certainly felt. She seemed attracted but also a bit guarded. He raised his eyebrows. "I felt a connection."

"Are you hooking up?"

"I'm meeting her at the library tomorrow. To do some research."

DeAngelo high-fived him. "Research! I like that."

Sam laughed. "Nothing like that! We're checking out some land-use records...."

DeAngelo interrupted. "You know, I've never seen you with a white girl!"

Sam considered his friend's statement. He had never sought out a white girl, or any girl for that matter. Instead, he relied on his friends to set him up on dates. If it happened, it happened. His closest companions were his books.

Sam shrugged. "None of the girls shared my passion for history or justice or even understood what I'm about."

DeAngelo scratched his head. "Well, good luck."

"What do you mean?"

"You're so damn smart," answered DeAngelo. "Your brain goes everywhere. People can't keep up with you. And you can be so intense!"

"How so?"

"You're always talking about some revolutionary philosopher or other."

DeAngelo spoke the truth. In University, Sam discovered the black nationalism of Marcus Garvey, the black self-empowerment of Booker T. Washington, the pan-Africanism of W.E.B. DuBois and even read biographies of Moses Tsembe, the Congolese revolutionary who fought the Belgians.

"Especially that guy from the Caribbean who went to Africa."

Sam picked up the paperback from his desk. "You mean Frantz Fanon?"

"Yeah. That guy! What's so great about him?"

Sam laughed. Fanon remained his favorite because of the depth of his analysis. Fanon studied psychiatry, and his analysis of black history and colonialism went deeper than mere material and social inquiry—he put the black person on a psychiatrist's couch and analyzed his psyche. "His writings influenced people around the world. Did you know that Huey Newton, the founder of the Black Panther Party, incorporated many of Fanon's ideas in the Party's manifesto?"

DeAngelo shook his head. "I don't know anything about that."

Sam recognized DeAngelo's disinterest. He changed the subject. "How's your girlfriend?" he asked, glancing up. *How does DeAngelo do it, sticking with the same girl he met as a junior in high school?* DeAngelo lived in the present. In a way, he envied his friend. It must be easy to be so singular in thought and undisturbed by the past.

"My lady? She's great. Can't wait to graduate and return home to her instead of spending time apart."

Sam's thoughts returned to Chantley. He certainly looked forward to meeting her again. *Did a future with her exist? How far would they go? Could he be like DeAngelo and find the right one?* He shook his head. He was getting ahead of himself. Just because he felt intensely attracted didn't mean it would turn out differently.

DeAngelo yawned. "You wanna hit the sack?"

Sam lay on his bed and stretched out his feet. "Yeah, sure."

DeAngelo turned off the light.

Chapter Three

Chantley met Sam at the university the following day. Her knees weakened, and as her heart pounded, she retreated into an emotional stiffness, a self-conscious distancing, like a young girl facing her first crush. Sam laughed. *He must know I like him. Am I being that obvious?* Yet, he said nothing. *A doubt crossed her mind. Maybe he isn't attracted to me. Perhaps I'm imagining the whole thing.* Still, it was considerate of him to continue helping her.

They headed to the main library. All metal and glass, it resembled nothing Chantley had seen at the Women's College. For her, a library meant a place to meet with teachers and fellow students in a simple setting, surrounded by shelves of dusty books. With its ever-present computer terminals, this shiny structure shielded students from each other, hindering the single most important mode of learning: discussion.

Sam knew his way around. He led her to the microfiche section and tracked the Land Use records. The answer immediately appeared. "When Boulder went through its renovation period, a lot of the downtown area was torn up and replaced with new structures," he informed her.

"The building my mother stayed in doesn't exist anymore?"

"I'm afraid so."

"Are there any other options?"

"Let's check the phone records. Maybe she moved to another part of town." Sam looked up. "What's your mother's name?"

"My dad's name is Armstrong, but they never formally married. Her name is Julia Flynn."

The search led to no new clues. "Your mother's phone records end abruptly. Many people stopped using landlines and switched to cell phones then." He raised his eyebrows. "She may have also moved out of Colorado."

"Isn't there anything you can do?" she questioned.

"Do you know anything else about your mother? Any relatives?"

"Yes! My mom's parents. She told me they're from Pittsburgh."

"I'm sure I can look up that name from the Pittsburgh phone records." A search produced forty-five Flynns. "Let me print this for you."

Chantley went to the printer and returned with the list. She felt stunned as she examined it, sensing the bottom fall beneath her. Did any of these Flynns have anything to do with her mother and, thus, with her hopes of settling down in America? Yet, it didn't surprise her. It had always been a long shot. She gazed into the distance, tears moistening her eyes.

Sam tapped her on her shoulder. "Come. Let's get a coffee," he said gently. She hesitated momentarily, then accepted. She could use the sympathy. She folded the list into the tin box, closed the lid and returned it to her bag.

They walked to the ground floor of the Student Center, found a coffee shop, brought their brews and occupied a small table in a corner. With the change to a less formal setting, not to mention having spent the entire morning with Sam, Chantley relaxed.

"What are you going to do?' asked Sam. He tapped the floor lightly with his right heel. Maybe it indicated nervousness or, possibly, excitement; she couldn't decide. His glasses, in strong dark frames, gave him a sense of intellectual solidity—the appearance of a man who thought things through. She found it reassuring.

"I could always go to Pittsburgh." Chantley shrugged. "And visit those addresses, talk to neighbors and so on. That may be the only way for me to locate my mom or her relatives." She dropped her eyes. "If she or they still exist." She could always return to

India. Yet, it seemed more of a dead-end than ever. Even if she went, what could she go back to?

"Take your time," cautioned Sam. "Pittsburgh's a long way from here."

Chantley pursed her lips. She didn't want to decide in haste, but the pressure of time and money weighed on her mind. She had already spent close to a week at Candace's stately home. And all her converted rupees amounted to just two hundred and fifty dollars. "Yes," she agreed, "that's good advice."

An awkward silence ensued. With the end of the chat, Chantley didn't know what to add. She glanced at her watch.

"Did you attend college in India?" Sam asked, changing the conversation, seemingly recognizing her discomfort.

She nodded her head.

"What did you study?"

"Philosophy." She shrugged her shoulders. "I should have gone into the sciences like all my classmates, but growing up in an ashram, I guess I've always liked that subject."

Sam laughed expansively. It embraced her in its warmth. "And I'm the king of lost causes, studying American History. I don't know how either of us will find real employment."

"Aren't you looking for a job?"

Sam rubbed his face with open palms. "I'm trying. I've sent out applications since the beginning of the semester." He gazed at the ceiling for several seconds. "But a job seems so far away."

"What do you mean?"

"I really don't know where I am at. I'm twenty-five, have an old car, not much money, no job and," he glanced at her, "no girlfriend."

Chantley grinned. His expression revealed a not-unexpected interest in her. "Don't worry," she reassured him, "things will work out."

"That's the problem. I don't think they will."

"Why not?"

"Getting a job would be great, but the problem is, I don't know what I want; or where I fit in."

"In what way?"

"I don't see myself stuck in a corporate job for the rest of my life. Especially with everything so messed up in this country. Am I supposed to kiss ass and become a cog in this broken system?" he asked, with more than a hint of anger.

Chantley knotted her eyebrows and glanced questioningly at him.

"This economic system is purely exploitative," he lectured. "We have to work our butts off at a barely livable wage so the elite can get wealthier. That's what getting a job means in America." He paused. "And since the whole system is based on exploitation, the way to get ahead is to become a part of the system and exploit others."

"Aren't you being pessimistic?" she questioned.

"No," he said firmly, his voice louder. "It's worse than that. Not only is America exploitative, but also racist. The types of jobs, the career opportunities, and the level of pay have a lot to do with skin color. The entire system is rigged against you, and all your efforts won't change a thing." Sam became more animated. "America sucks."

Chantley didn't know what to say. His rejection of all things American surprised her. Everyone she knew in India wanted to come over. In some ways, she understood the ambition: migrating to America meant beating the odds and gaining passage to a world where riches and opportunity awaited. But it ignored large parts of reality. In India, American racism and poverty, though briefly acknowledged, didn't taint the golden tale of American enterprise, even if some Indians became its victims. The narratives revolved around those who had made it, whereas the stories of those who didn't—the poorly-paid restaurant workers, the abandoned homemakers, the unsuccessful businessmen—were dismissed, in fact, seen as personal failures. No one discussed the disappointment, indeed the shame, of the unsuccessful.

Yet, here was the voice of someone who plainly laid out the faults and exposed the warts of the American dream. In contrast to the folklore, did America benefit only the privileged and the landed, but not every newcomer who arrived on its shores? Did this country represent every immigrant's dream, or did nightmares unfold? Sam's description of America jarred her ideations. She, too, in one sense, had flown to America in search of fulfillment. But did she err in coming?

"Don't you think that things can change?" she asked.

Sam nodded his head vigorously. "Now that's something I'm interested in doing—changing things. I don't know how long America can keep going the same way. The system's violence is astounding—we're continuously at war around the world, destroying the earth and exploiting the poor both at home and abroad."

Chantley absorbed this for a few seconds. Sam's profound analysis of his situation and American culture felt incomplete, being descriptive but not prescriptive. "How do you change things?"

"According to Frantz Fanon, the entire racist structure has to be dismantled, violently if necessary."

She looked at him in alarm.

"The problem is, where to start?" He stared at her. "Maybe the first thing is to go back to the beginning and see where all this mess started."

He was right about that. "Everyone acts according to their karma," she offered. "Maybe even entire nations."

Sam cut her off. "What can you say about a country that starts its history with slavery and genocide? What kind of karma is that?"

Chapter Four

On the third day, Sam and Chantley sat on a park bench, watching children play on a bright yellow play set. He noticed things about her: the light fuzz under her earlobes visible only when the sun shone indirectly on her face; the thin ring of hazel circling her green irises and her self-effacing, shy laughter. He explored her with as much interest as a traveler would a strange new continent. Sam enjoyed her company and, despite realizing her future remained uncertain and their acquaintance a dead end, went with the flow. Apparently, Boulder would be just a stop, a transit point, in her journey; yet he realized she needed the time to build up her confidence and gain the courage to move on.

Chantley had her shoulder bag with her.

"You carry that with you everywhere, don't you?"

Chantley nodded her head. "I have some important things in it," she replied. "Just sentimental stuff."

"Like what?"

Chantley set it on her lap and proceeded to open it. Sam noticed that her middle and ring fingers were the same length on both hands. Strange, he thought, but said nothing.

She pulled out the tin box. Sam recognized it from their first meeting. "I keep some papers in there." She set it aside and then retrieved a small blue cloth tie-bag.

The tie-bag intrigued him. "What's in it?"

Chantley opened it and, reaching in, pulled out a palmful of tiny stones. She lined them on the bench and proceeded to detail their histories. "I like to collect pebbles from all the places I visit."

She pointed to a tiny brown sandstone. "I picked this one up in Haridwar, on the side of the Ganges, four years ago." She picked up its neighbor, a bit of white quartz. "And this one comes from the southern tip of India, a place known as Kanyakumari. It was given to me by my father." Each minuscule pebble, its individuality revealed by its particular narrative, had stayed etched in her memory.

"How long have you been doing this?"

"Since I was twelve."

Sam's eyes rounded, and his mouth dropped. It was an utterly charming pastime, completely childlike. Beneath this twenty-one-year-old woman's body, sculpted by years of yoga, behind the bright, intelligent eyes, hid a still-young girl. A surge of protectiveness overcame him. *I need to take care of her.* American culture—its internal codes of behavior and conversation, the understanding of the local idiom—surely perplexed her. Like any visitor, she needed someone through whose eyes she could discern the cultural landscape. And she needed comfort.

She put her things away. "Are you from here?" she asked.

"Denver, actually." He snickered.

"What?" she questioned him.

"Just remembering old times."

She eyed him curiously.

"I grew up in a rough neighborhood," he explained. "I started skipping classes in Middle School. High school was terrible. I hated all my subjects. I couldn't figure out how any of the stuff I learned had any relevance."

Sam tapped his right heel against the ground. It had started with his family: his father had left after months of arguments when Sam was just ten. Strangely the disagreements weren't with Ma but with Grandma. Being abandoned filled Sam with anger. He took it out on other kids and against the adult world. "I got into fights and started stealing things."

Chantley shot him a startled look. "My God! A thief," she exclaimed.

He cracked a smile. Her alarm seemed childlike. Obviously, she grew up sheltered.

"I can't imagine doing anything like that," she continued. "I'm terrified of the police. In India, they publicly beat suspects in marketplaces with thick bamboo rods. Sometimes they take bribes to arrest people or to keep them in jail."

Sam was taken aback but continued. "I spent my teenage years learning how to survive, getting an education on the streets, figuring out who to trust and how to take care of myself. I saw my friends getting shot or going to prison. Victims in many ways, but they didn't recognize that. They thought they were free—to chase money, women, and cars—but never understood why things turned out the way they did. They never had a chance."

Those were tough years. No clear path to the future opened. He had to grow up fast and learn hard lessons on survival. Many of his friends got lost at that time. Landing in the county jail and meetings with several of his old middle-school friends proved to be an unsettling experience. A nicer kid than his best friend Emmanuel didn't exist. But in the prison cafeteria, a different young man showed up. His eyes displayed incomprehension; he didn't understand what had happened to him. When Emmanuel confessed to not expecting to live past twenty, Sam remembered reacting with shock—he recognized himself in his friend.

"Then what happened?"

"My grandmother. She whupped my ass with a switch after I spent a month in jail for stealing. I was lucky: the city attorney appreciated my grandmother's attitude. She gave him her word that she'd keep me straight." He grimaced at the thought of his grandma. She maintained a tough, leather-like personality since he first remembered her. Being abandoned by her husband had soured her on life. Sam shook his head. After a while, living with her wore him down. That's why he moved to Boulder. He needed the space to spread his wings, to open his mind.

His mother was different. Despite her husband also leaving her, she channeled her energy into raising him and into her church. She never let bitterness into her heart. Instead, she recognized his native intelligence and need for direction. "One day, my mother sat me down and told me an education is important because you need one to understand your rights and where you come from." Her advice came from a gentler place and was thus easier to accept.

It opened his eyes and gave him a ladder to climb. "I realized I had to learn my history and civil liberties to ensure my place in society and get justice. Now this, I related to—something that got me enthusiastic."

Chantley nodded her head. "That's where your interest in Black History comes from."

"That's right."

"How did you get into University?"

"After jail, I got a job at a convenience store and found out about a program that helps dropouts get their high school diplomas after a couple of years. I got top marks in the state on my GED exams and a scholarship to C.U. I read every book I could lay my hands on." The radical writers opened his eyes and sparked a fire in his mind. He didn't have to be stuck. They illuminated paths to follow.

Several drops of rain interrupted his thoughts. "Sometimes we get a good spring storm," said Sam, glancing up.

"This reminds me of the rainy season back home," she said. "I'm just soaking it in."

"Your skin looks creamy. You're glowing!" The unexpected humidity brightened her skin and reddened her expressive lips.

Chantley straightened her now-curly hair and pushed it behind her ears. "We should get out of here before it starts pouring," she said.

"How about lunch? It's eleven-thirty."

"Where?"

"Remember that Mexican restaurant on Pearl Street? We passed it a couple of times. I can smell those spices!"

"I'm not that hungry," she replied, looking away.

Her reply puzzled Sam. They had spent the entire morning together, and neither had a bite to eat.

"Mexican cooking is just like Indian," assured Sam. "You'll love this place."

"I don't know," she mumbled, clutching her handbag.

"I insist." Is she shy or tight on funds?

Chantley surrendered. "Sure. I appreciate your friendship. And I'm hungry."

As soon as they got up, more drops fell, and when they reached his car, it rained steadily.

They parked in front of Las Tres Madres, situated in a single-storied, red-brick building with a giant neon sign on the roof depicting three Mexican women, one dressed in a long red gown, the second in a white one and the third in green, all with sombreros on their head and exaggerated smiles on their faces. The unexpected shower turned into a thunderstorm and plunged the temperature by fifteen degrees in minutes. As they rushed inside, the heavens opened up. He shivered.

They found a table pushed up against the large front window from where Boulderites, ill-prepared for the unanticipated downpour, could be seen rushing indoors. A young waitress came by with a large one-sheet menu encased in thick plastic, showing pictures of different dishes, each accompanied by their names, prices and one-line descriptions listing their ingredients. Everything looked incredibly delicious.

Sam immediately knew what he wanted. He sat back and waited for Chantley. After a lengthy study, Chantley spoke. "I'm unfamiliar with this cuisine, but the burrito looks good. I'm accustomed to the rice, beans, and vegetables, and the bread resembles a chapatti."

"Great," said Sam, "but how about enchiladas?"

"What's that?"

"Corn tortillas, stuffed, smothered with a chili sauce and baked with cheese on top and they're served sizzling on an iron plate. You'll love it!" He pointed to its picture on the menu.

"Isn't the burrito good?" she questioned.

Sam shook his head. As her guide, he had to help her. "That's a good choice, but I'm familiar with Mexican food, having grown up here. In weather like this, nice hot enchiladas will warm you up like nothing else."

Chantley wrinkled her nose as if to say, 'you're like most men who think they always know better.' Her reaction startled him. He was only trying to help. He struggled to think of what to say.

"How about we order both?" she suggested. "And we can share."

"Great idea!"

Chantley giggled. Sam sheepishly joined her laughter.

Chapter Five

On Sunday morning, Chantley met Sam at the Mall.

"Wanna go to a football game?" he asked.

She checked her watch. It read ten-thirty. "When is that?'

"At noon."

"Sure."

"It's the last game of the season."

They arrived at Folsom Field, at the University of Colorado campus, at eleven-thirty and drove into the parking lot in his brown two-door Chevy coupe. As anticipation filled the air, thousands of people streamed into the stadium, dressed in gold and black. Sam led her to their seats, halfway up, in the stadium's middle.

"These are the best seats," he explained. "Better than ground level. From here, you can see the entire football field."

The stands, packed with screaming fans, the spectacle of the marching band, the somersaulting cheerleaders and the students' energy, all amazed her. When the field finally cleared, the players, wearing strange outfits with helmets covering their heads, ran onto the field. The crowd roared and jumped to its feet. Chantley hesitantly stood up and looked around.

With a strange-shaped ball being kicked down the field, the game started. Apparently, the game revolved around this object, which the men ran with, kicked or caught. The most important people on the field were several men with striped shirts. Each time they blew their whistles, everyone fell and, bizarrely enough, ignored the ball, which, the instant before, they had savagely fought over.

"What's happening?" she asked.

"Each team has eleven players." Sam pointed to solid lines at the end of each side of the field. "The goal is to cross those lines with the ball. Each time a team does that, it's called a touchdown."

One of the players took the ball and heaved it down the field. As soon as another player caught it, one of the striped-shirt men blew his whistle, and everyone fell down. Sometimes the fellow who initially got the ball would forget to throw it, and another player would grab the ball from his hands and start running. Instantly, everyone from both teams would run after the poor fellow, catch him, throw him on the ground and jump on top. After enough players, usually, nine or ten, piled on, a whistle blew. Collective amnesia would sweep the players, even the fellow at the bottom, as everyone got up and walked away, leaving the ball lying on the field.

"That's not fair," she commented.

"What?" asked Sam.

"Don't you see? They always make the smallest players run with the ball. And all the big men fall on top of him."

Sam laughed out loud. "That's his job. He's the half-back."

"And who's the one who keeps getting the ball shoved into his hands?"

"That's the quarterback."

"You have a quarterback and a half-back?"

"Yes. Sometimes you also have a full-back."

The math didn't add up. "So, you have a quarterback, a half-back and a fullback. Then you must have a three-quarter back?"

Sam bellowed with laughter. "There's nothing called a three-quarter back. Sometimes, you have two half-backs on a play."

Do two half-backs equal one fullback? And can two quarterbacks take the place of one half-back? She hesitated but kept the thought to herself. She didn't want to add to Sam's mirth. More questions arose. "Why does one team have a quarterback when the other doesn't?"

"What do you mean?"

"Look," she said, pointing at the field. "One team has a man throwing the ball, but the other doesn't."

Sam guffawed. "You want the two offenses on the field at the same time?"

She scrunched her eyebrows. "I have no idea what you're saying."

"See, here's what happens. Each offense keeps the ball for four downs. If they can't get ten yards, they have to give up the ball."

Four downs? Oh yes, a down happens every time the players fall down. So if a team falls four times, they must give up the ball. She wrinkled her forehead. What a strange game!

The more she thought about football, the less sense it made. It was the most confounding, illogical game anyone could make up. The entire affair felt rather dull-headed. The action lasted for mere seconds, while the rest of the time, the players stood around with their hands on their hips or gathered in a circle, bent at their waists, and embarrassingly enough, pushing their enormous buttocks up in the air. She lost interest in the whole thing.

Instead, she gazed at Sam as the action absorbed his interest. She measured him: she reached his shoulders. He projected strength and vigor. His companionship energized her and made her feel alive.

Finally, after about an hour, the teams evacuated the field.

"Half-time," said Sam.

Thank God. I'm getting bored.

"Enjoying yourself?"

"Oh yes!" she lied brightly. "I'm having a wonderful time!" She leaned against him as he put his left arm around her shoulders and nestled his head against hers. She reveled in the moment. When did she feel like this before? Of course! When Vijay, for the first time, held her hand as they walked down the hill from the ashram to the village. That moment of first contact with a man—that tingling down her spine, the turning feeling in her chest, the bated breath and thumping heart, the wonder of discovering someone was interested in her—had opened her to the possibility of romantic love.

Sam drew a deep breath. "Your hair smells beautiful," he remarked. "What is it?"

"I use pure coconut oil on my hair," she replied.

"Oh, yes! I recognize the scent."

She closed her eyes. Did she open up to Sam so unhesitatingly because she had trod this path before with Vijay? Vijay lured her out of her girlishness, yet, with her painful shyness, it remained a wonder they came so close to marriage. Still, their ship crashed on the rocks of family acceptance.

Did another path, trod before, exist? One traveled with Sam? The sensation upon first sighting Sam; that feeling of timelessness, of unreality, of being locked in a theater which endlessly replayed her life on celluloid, reappeared. She felt desolate. *How I wish I could give meaning to this feeling, this mystery!* She rubbed her forehead. *It won't go away; the longer I'm with Sam, the stronger it's becoming.* She opened her mouth to speak but didn't feel comfortable bringing up the subject of karma. Sam didn't believe in reincarnation. *Most likely, he'll think me strange.* She pursed her lips. *I'll just wait till the correct time.*

The second half began, and Sam's focus returned to the action on the field. Despite his occasional explanations, she completely lost interest. Instead, her thoughts turned to her mother.

Chantley remembered waking one morning in the winter at the ashram when fog enveloped the hills, bringing discomfort and a cold humidity. Their place was a mess. Clothes littered the corners of the empty house; blankets lay on the floor, and doors were left flung open. She had waddled to the toilet at the house's back and found her father arguing with her mother, who had locked herself inside. After many minutes of back and forth, of pleading and cajoling, her father had stormed away. Chantley remembered waiting outside, hungry and shivering, in tears, for what seemed, at that time, forever. When the door finally opened, she rushed in. Her mother picked her up and held her tight against her bosom. "I'm so sorry," she said, over and over, with tears streaming from her eyes.

Chantley didn't understand, at that age, what the apology meant. Did her mother express regret for making her wait outside, arguing with her father or being lonely? Did it foreshadow the more serious and deeper withdrawal? But at that moment, her mother's embrace meant comfort. Chantley remembered how close she felt to her mother then, one of the few times they clearly bonded and, after her mother left, of much she yearned for that same sense of refuge.

Finally, the game ended. Sam stood on his feet, shouting enthusiastically, while she filled her lungs with relief. They followed the crowd out of the stadium.

"How did you like it?" he asked.

"Very exciting," she replied.

"What part did you like most?"

Her face went blank. *What am I supposed to say?* She had to pick something that would show her interest but, at the same time, not expose her ignorance.

"I like the uniforms," she mumbled. "Very colorful."

He looked at her with askance. "That's it? The uniforms?"

She struggled. She had to come up with something else. "That buffalo that ran down the field," she remarked. "I like animals."

Sam laughed. "The mascot?"

She had to change the topic. "The best part is being with you," she said, smiling.

Sam beamed. "You're right! Being with you is the best part!"

Chapter Six

They joined the queue streaming out of the stadium to the parking lot. The women, mostly dressed in tight tees and shorts exposing their long legs, and the men, in blue jeans and khaki baseball caps adorned with the University's logo, jostled each other as they excitedly crowded out of the stadium. The students celebrated the home team's win. Cheers and hollers punctuated the bright afternoon air. Ten minutes later, Sam and Chantley squeezed through a gate and entered the parking lot.

As the crowd filled the lot, many cars exited, but a large number sat in place, dotting the black asphalt like little metal islands, surrounded by yellow folding lawn chairs, small gray tables holding cases of beer and even barbeques roasting hot dogs. And everywhere, a cacophony of music—classic rock, synthetic techno, but mostly hip-hop—blasted from assorted car radios, boom boxes and even from huge speakers built into modified car trunks.

Sam glanced at Chantley. She looked confused. "What's the matter?" he asked.

"I'm not used to this," she answered, sidling up to him. "It's a bit strange." The public consumption of liquor and the whooping and exaggerated behavior of the crowd startled her. He reached over and held her hand. She didn't resist.

"I'm used to crowds," she explained. "But the way people are behaving here is very foreign to me." Sam searched the parking lot. Being among the last to arrive, his car rested at the far end. They would have to navigate their way through the celebrating crowd.

Somewhere in the middle of the lot, they passed five young men leaning against the side of an old beat-up black Ford with a couple of cases of beer on its hood. Sam and Chantley had no choice but to cross the men to reach their vehicle. A tall skinny man in rumpled clothing leaned against the Ford. "Hey, babe. How you doing?" He waved a can of beer at Chantley.

Several hoots from the other men followed. Sam felt Chantley's grip tightening on his hand.

"Ignore them," he said. "They're drunk."

The man stepped in front of Sam. "Hey, how 'bout sharing her with us?" His friends laughed at his bravado. "She's a real babe."

Sam shook his head and attempted to walk around him. The man, egged on by his friends, didn't stop. Instead, he grabbed Chantley's arm. "Come on, sweetheart, give me some."

With round, startled eyes, she gaped at him. Sam pulled her back.

"Leave her alone," he warned. "She's mine."

"With you?" The drunk let loose a long whistle. "What's a pretty girl like that doing with a man like you?"

Sam immediately recognized the comment's context. What's a black man like you doing with a white woman? He frowned, and the sinews in his forearm hardened.

"Let's get out of here," whispered Chantley.

"Get lost," said Sam derisively to the drunk.

"Oooh." The men moved closer and faked fear at these words. Their actions challenged the man gripping Chantley's arm to persist. The man hesitated as a glimmer of common sense appeared in his eyes, recognizing that further action would escalate the situation. But his drunken friends egged him on.

"What you gonna do?" they shouted. "You're gonna let him get away with that?"

Sam lost his temper. He pulled away from Chantley. He remembered something he had read. Che Guevara had written about the importance of shooting the first man in a column of soldiers. The rest would lose courage. He tightened his hands into fists and squared up against the man. "I'm gonna kick your ass."

Chantley grabbed Sam's arm. He looked at her panicked face. *I need to get her away. The poor girl is terrified.* He stepped away from the bully and attempted to lead her away from danger. But risking humiliation from his friends, the man picked up a can of beer from the car's hood. Shaking it vigorously, he popped it open, spraying warm beer over Sam and Chantley. She screamed.

Sam punched the man in the chest. He staggered back and slammed against the car. His four friends, swearing, their faces contorting with anger, jumped in front, ready to attack Sam. Sam pushed a crying Chantley behind him and raised his fists.

"Help," yelled Chantley. "Please help!"

Immediately, a dozen people from close-by cars rushed over. Admonishing all concerned, the crowd pulled the men apart and, in seconds, restored order. Sam grabbed Chantley's arm and quickly led her away. Within minutes, they reached his car. He leaned against the front driver's door as sweat ran down his face and glanced at her. She still shook.

Sam took a deep breath. His eyes cleared. "You're terrified, aren't you?"

"Of course," she replied, with tears still trickling down her face. "Weren't you?"

"Those punks? Not a chance." Sam wanted to smile but kept a straight face for her sake. He had faced much greater threats than these college boys. He curled his fingers into fists and brought them to his face like a boxer in a ring. "I've seen worse."

"They really frightened me."

Sam straightened up and pulled her close. "I'm sorry," he said. "It happens. They're just a bunch of drunk college kids."

He embraced her, and after several minutes, she stopped shaking, and her breathing eased.

"Thank you," she said finally. "I'm so glad you're here."

He comforted her. "Don't worry. Anytime you need me, let me know."

They got into his car, and Chantley pushed herself next to him and entwined her fingers, white-knuckled, with his right hand. As they drove, she closed her eyes.

"We're here," he said.

"Already?" she asked. She opened her eyes. They had stopped in front of her friend's house in Upper Boulder Canyon.

"We've been on the road for the past half-hour. Get a good night of sleep."

She reached over and embraced him tightly. "Thanks. I'm grateful."

*****

As she lay in bed, all her insecurities turned into sharp focus. The shocking experience of the day unsettled her, yet her heart filled with thankfulness for Sam. Her chest glowed warmly as his face came into her mind's view. She felt a powerful urge to call him.

She sat up in alarm. What am I doing? Didn't I commit to not getting close to Sam? Or am I on a slide, inexorably going down? She painfully admitted that he meant nothing in the overall scheme of things. She had to search for her mother in Pittsburgh but couldn't imagine setting out alone to the other side of the continent.

What is Sam to me? She shook her head. *I can't fall in love with him. But, until I leave town, I have to treat him like a friend and ensure that it remains that way.* With that decision, she breathed deeply, relaxed, and closed her eyes.

Sam phoned a couple of times over the next few days, but she resisted the temptation and spent the time reading in her room or renewing her yoga practice with Candace on the deck.

Chapter Seven

Sam looked at his cell phone. Should I call Chantley again? He rubbed his forehead. He didn't want to appear persistent, but he hadn't seen her in almost a week. Alarmingly, she hadn't taken his calls.

Is she so sensitive that she would hide in the hills after the incident at the football game? Had the episode frightened her so much? He reflected for a moment. Of course! No violent confrontations could have occurred at the ashram.

Indeed, her insecurity, coupled with cultural differences, came into play. She had hardly any money and fewer friends. Aren't we just friends? He shook his head. The idea felt false. He was falling fast in love, unlike any relationship he'd experienced before.

Sam gazed out the window. The Saturday morning proved to be a beauty, a great day to be in the country. He glanced at his phone again. *I'll call her one more time.*

*****

Chantley rubbed her chin. Should I go? What's the point of pursuing a friendship that will end soon enough? Her mind resisted, but she accepted the invitation anyway. After all, her only other option meant sitting alone in her room, feeling uneasy about taking advantage of her friend's goodwill for another day.

The Saturday morning warmed up early, and she met him in front of the bus station in Boulder, the ride down from the hills having taken just twenty minutes. They took off in his car and drove west on Interstate 70 toward Idaho Springs, which Sam described as an old mining town turned tourist trap. It offered visitors a chance to wander cobblestoned streets to shop, dine, or even pan for gold at its now-defunct mine on the side of Clear Creek.

As the elevation increased, the temperature freshened, and Chantley's spirits revived. She felt at home in the hills, though the ones in Colorado featured pines and birches rather than the more familiar old-growth tropical forest. After a couple of hours, they reached their destination. The weekend brought out the tourists who constantly crossed the little town's narrow streets in colorful clothes, resembling butterflies flitting about tree branches.

They walked into a tiny corner store selling crystals and inexpensive jewelry.

"Hi, Sam," said a blue-eyed, gray-haired lady from behind the counter.

"This is Joanna," Sam introduced Chantley. "She owns the store. Joanna, this is Chantley." Joanna said hello and smiled mischievously at Sam. She lifted a small flat lapis-lazuli pendant on a silver chain from the counter. "How about this for your friend?" She passed him the pendant.

Chantley blushed. The only man who ever offered her gifts previously was Vijay, and she certainly hadn't come to America to become romantically involved, despite her budding feelings for Sam. She silently shook her head. Sam nodded. They quickly left the shop as Joanna suppressed her laughter.

The town's central area, consisting of perhaps six or seven streets, packed shoulder-to-shoulder with curio shops, cafes and restaurants, took less than an hour to explore. "Shall we hike in the hills above town," Sam asked.

"Of course."

They returned to the automobile and headed off. After half an hour, Sam pulled into a parking area on the side of the road where a trail climbing into the hills existed. Spring had arrived in the Rockies, and the melting snow dripped on stone, gathered in ribbons of water and collected into streams and waterfalls gushing down the slopes. After fifteen minutes of hiking, they came across a creek racing between stones, bordered by spruce, coursing down the hillside.

"Hey, let's check this out," he said.

Check this out? Another bit of American idiom she couldn't identify. "What do you mean?"

"Let's explore it," he replied, pointing to the stream.

"Sure. Where do you want to go?"

"Up the stream."

"Up the stream? How do we do that?"

"Follow me."

Sam jumped on a rock in the rushing water. Chantley followed. He hopped from stone to stone, careful not to get wet. She followed his lead until they reached a ten-foot-high, dark-gray boulder that split the stream in two.

"Let's climb up," he offered.

She hesitated. "I don't know."

"Don't worry. I'll show you."

Sam scaled the rock, his shoes nestling against tiny cracks, his strong arms pulling him up to the top.

"I can't do that," Chantley protested. "I'm not as strong as you."

"I'll help you."

Sam lay on his stomach on the boulder's smooth top and, holding her hands, pulled her up as her feet discovered tiny indentations in the stone. When she joined him on the summit, Chantley beamed with excitement.

"What a view!" she exclaimed, surprised at the height attained in just thirty minutes. Far below, their automobile, parked on a tiny, circular strip of black pavement hugging the outside edge of a cliff, resembled an impossibly-small brown matchbox and, many hundreds of feet beyond, speckled by both bright sunlight and dark shadow, lay the deep valley where the creek snaked, shining prismatically in the late-afternoon sun.

After admiring the view for several minutes, she closed her eyes and took a deep breath, the sweet air filling her lungs, the warm sun beaming on her face and the gentle breeze washing over her body like champagne.

Suddenly, she felt giddy. It might have been the thin air, or maybe her closed eyes made her lose her balance. She tipped to her right and felt herself slipping. She opened her eyes as the world tilted wildly. She screamed. Sam's strong arms instantly caught her. Electricity flashed through her. She gasped.

"Thank you," she whispered, pulling away, unable to stand his overpowering presence.

"You're welcome." He rubbed his forehead, puzzled. "What is it?"

"I...I'm shy," she admitted.

Sam laughed. "I like that." He held her hand. "And I like you."

Chantley's cheeks stained crimson.

When they climbed down and started the long drive back, evening had set. Chantley said nothing but felt enveloped in a warm coziness, experiencing immense satisfaction and a tingling in her fingers and toes. The ride felt magical, as if she were flying down to the plains in an airship, on the soft wings of inky darkness, the stars blinking in the sheer mountain air, and her heart a-flutter all the way back to Boulder.

*****

After two weeks, Chantley settled into a daily routine: yoga in the mornings with Candace, joined surprisingly by Charles, lunch with Sam, followed by afternoons spent together and evenings alone in her room.

Chapter Eight

Sam pulled into the driveway of the small cottage-style home in Aurora, a working-class suburb in East Denver. It sat in a small lot, edged by similar houses, all with cream-colored aluminum sidings, large bay windows in front, with concrete steps leading to front doors.

During his parents' generation, almost everyone made a living, however humble. Since then, the economy resembled waves on a beach, sometimes cresting and, at other times, hitting bottom. His generation found little financial stability.

He looked down the street. At the end stood a dusty little park where he had hung around with his unemployed, out-of-school friends. He remembered one day, at age fifteen, meeting three young men from outside the neighborhood come looking for a fight.

"You're a bunch of cockroaches," he had yelled at them. "You're all jumping me at the same time." He gave them an option. "I don't mind fighting all three of you separately." Sam smiled. He had whupped their asses, one by one. They never came back, and he gained his street cred. He wondered about the gang-bangers. Were they still alive?

The yard looked neat and the siding clean, but the roof needed replacing. A large elm tree grew in the front yard, shading the driveway. He got out and bounded up the steps to the front door. He didn't bother using the bell.

"Hey Sam," said Grandma as soon as he walked in. "What are you doing here? Don't you have your exams coming up?"

Sam grimaced. "You don't have to do that anymore," he said. She always kept him straight. She did that during high school and later when he studied for his GED. Now, it had become a reflex. "Aren't I doing well in all my courses?"

"Of course. But it doesn't hurt to check."

"I needed to take the afternoon off and relax a bit." He looked around. "Where's Ma?"

"The restaurant called her this morning and offered her an extra shift."

Sam felt disappointed. If he had known Ma wasn't home, he wouldn't have spontaneously dropped in. But it didn't surprise him. She always took extra shifts. It helped the family survive over the years.

"When's she coming home?"

"Soon. You hungry?" Grandma asked.

Sam checked his cell phone. "I'll wait until she's here."

He walked over and sat on the couch. The furniture—the cracked-leather sofa, the heavy wood-and-glass coffee table, the end tables—hadn't changed in twenty years. He couldn't remember how old the potted plants were but remembered seeing them on either side of the television stand for what seemed like forever. The fan whirred on the ceiling, dissipating the mid-day heat. It felt comfortable, like home.

His grandmother and mother made an odd pair. As cranky as the old lady was, his mother was equally affectionate. But they stuck with each other, as foils to the other's foibles. Their relationship worked. The two ladies got along and kept the old place clean and tidy.

Grandma sat on a side chair and picked up one of her fashion magazines, which she opened but did not read. "Anything going on?" she asked.

Sam hesitated. He needed someone to talk to, but would Grandma understand him? For her generation, a degree meant a ticket to a good life. He still felt vacant and aimless despite completing almost four years of undergraduate studies.

"I don't know what to do with my life."

Grandma picked up her glasses from the end table and slipped them on her nose. "What do you mean by that?"

He sighed. "I've been trying, but I don't have a job yet."

She glared at him. "Try harder."

He shrugged his shoulders. He just didn't have the enthusiasm. "I don't know what the point is. I don't know how I fit in, where I belong."

She shook her head. "Why can't you just concentrate on what you must do?"

"'A people without the knowledge of their history, origin and culture is like a tree without roots.' That's what Marcus Garvey said. And that's the way I feel, rootless."

"Marcus Garvey? Here you go again, with your head in the clouds."

Sam stopped. Bringing this up with her was a mistake. It reminded him of all the times they had argued before he left for Boulder. *There's no way she'll understand. She never reads anything philosophical.* "Yeah. I'll keep trying for a job," he said, to quiet her.

"Good," she said emphatically. "Anything else?"

"I met a girl in Boulder."

"Really? What's she like?"

"She's real nice. I liked her right away. She was hesitant in the beginning, but we've been hanging out for almost a month now."

"Where's she from?"

"She's American. But," he quickly added, "she grew up in India," as if the clarification would make Chantley more acceptable.

"India? Is she Indian?"

"No, she's white."

His Grandma gave him a stare. "I don't know about these students at the University. These girls in Boulder are all spoiled. They got these rich daddies and trust funds to take care of them."

Sam rubbed his head. Grandma was just starting. That was her first pitch. "Nah, I picked up that she isn't rich."

"What's the attraction? You never cared for white girls before."

Chantley was like a bird with a broken wing that fell at his feet. His help had been automatic; he didn't think about it. He was flattered she trusted him, that he had the opportunity to guide her. He remembered James Baldwin's description of life in France after the Second World War. While race defined almost every aspect of a black man's existence in America, it mattered not in France, especially in friendships with women. Chantley brought that type of goodness with her.

"She's different. She treats me like a regular person. There's no games or attitudes."

"Sam," she warned, "get away from that girl."

He knew Grandma's way of thinking. Being young, poor and having given birth to four children in five years, one his father, she had to sell the family land and resettle in Denver. The betrayal by her husband had bred a general distrust of white people. He sympathized. In his youth, he had adopted her resentment. His anger reflected hers until he channeled his energy into his studies. Then, he moved away from bitterness.

"Why should I?" he argued.

His grandma sighed. "You think everything's changed now. But it hasn't."

Sam knew what was coming. It had to be different in the 1940s when she married a white man. In those times, interracial marriage took guts, but obviously, his grandfather didn't have the gumption to stick around and make it last.

"We were a pretty normal family until your grandfather left. He caused a lot of damage, and we were never the same again." Sam knew she blamed her husband for what came afterward: being left destitute and her kids scattered to the winds.

"You'll regret it," she continued. "When she doesn't need you, she'll dump you."

"We're not serious," Sam explained. "She's just a friend."

His grandma wasn't fooled. "There's more to it than that. If you aren't serious, why did you bring it up? You hardly mentioned your previous girlfriends."

"Listen," he argued. "I'm not going to do anything stupid."

"Uh-huh," agreed Grandma. "Right now, you need to complete your studies, not chase after girls or keep thinking about this or that writer. You'll be the first one in the family to get a degree. Then, when you get a good job, you can do what you want. But don't lose track of your goals."

Sam looked at her worn, wrinkled face and thinning white hair. A blue ring of age edged her brown pupils, and her hands shook unsteadily. But her voice was clear. She showed no hesitation. When the family around her crumbled, she had stood strong. He had to admit he wouldn't be where he was without her.

"Don't worry, Grandma, I'll do the right thing."

The door opened, and his mother walked in, dressed in her blue restaurant outfit and tennis flats. She smiled upon seeing him. She was one of the most even-tempered people he knew. It's interesting how two people sharing the same fate could be so different. Despite also losing her husband, his mother hadn't descended into anger. Instead, she fully accepted her fate and deepened her attachments to what she had left: her child and her church. She held no grudges against neither her husband nor her mother-in-law. When she wasn't working or cooking, she helped at the church--a good, hard-working Christian woman. She came over and hugged him.

"Ma, you changed your hair," he remarked. She had it straightened, and it lay in a short bob along the sides of her head.

"You like it?" she asked.

"Yeah, I've never seen it like that before."

She went to the fridge and brought out the food to be heated on the stove. Working at the restaurant made her a bit heavy but also strong. As she set the table, Grandma filled in the details of Sam's new friend.

Ma was shocked. "You're going out with a white girl?"

Sam laughed. He knew her reaction came not from distrust but surprise. "Aren't you the one who keeps telling me Christ's love is for all his children?"

"Absolutely! And I expect you to treat everyone you meet with respect! But you never told me you had a girlfriend."

Maybe I shouldn't have brought this up. It's way too premature. "She's not my girlfriend. Just someone I met recently."

"You've never stuck with any girl for long," said Ma. "It's like you can't find the one that fits you."

Sam shrugged. Maybe he wasn't ready for anyone before. Perhaps, this time, it would be different.

"Tell me about her."

"She's from India. She's real nice."

"India?" questioned his mother. He could tell she was trying to place it on a map.

"Whatever brought you two together?" she questioned.

"Chantley thinks we know each other from a previous life."

Ma scrunched her eyebrows together. "What do you mean?"

"You know, reincarnation."

"Reincarnation!" she exclaimed. "That ain't Christian!"

Sam guffawed.

Chapter Nine

Chantley picked out a world atlas from the bookshelf at the University Library. The past several weeks had clarified that, despite her knowledge of the language, albeit in a more formal, almost British way, her understanding of American culture and idiom remained far from satisfactory. Most students spoke slang, and their colloquialisms remained hard to understand. What did 'from a horse's mouth' mean? What about 'from left field'? She leaned on Sam for understanding, and he gladly obliged.

She joined Sam, where he sat with his textbooks sprawled out. Exams had started, but Sam seemed far more interested in coaching her on aspects of American language and customs instead of studying. In College, exams had occupied her with anxiety; Sam's casual approach filled her with wonder. Either he displayed supreme confidence or was well on his way to failing all his courses.

She opened the book to the center page, and a map of America stared back. She remembered seeing the same in a child's atlas in India and marveling at the large squares that delineated the different states as if drawn with a pencil and ruler—so different from the states in India, all defined by squiggly lines that followed rivers, mountains or the invisible borders of language and ethnicity.

"She's such a big country," said Chantley.

Sam cocked his head. "Interesting. You addressed America in the feminine."

Chantley looked up. It had been purely reflexive. "Yes. But isn't the Earth our mother?" Bhumi mata: Mother earth. That's how Indians addressed the planet. Or Bharat mata: Mother India.

"Isn't it anthropomorphic to give personhood to an object, especially one as big as a country? America is a piece of land, part of the North American continent."

Chantley touched her fingers to her lips. She recollected Guru-ji's teachings. He taught that the Universe's real nature, called Prakriti, was eternally spiritual while the visible material world, though also real, was only the temporary manifestation of that original condition. He also taught that both the material and the spiritual universes were full of personalities, some human and others not.

"The land is not a person in the human sense," she replied. "But looking at countries as organic, living things can be useful, even if you don't accept the premise. People change over time and adopt different beliefs. Similarly, in nations, certain ideas become influential while others fade away. Sometimes these ideas are life-affirming and allow for growth, but, on other occasions, nations adopt beliefs that are so poisonous it destroys them."

"That's a useful way of looking at it. Perhaps countries need psychoanalysis as much as individuals. I've wondered why ideas like genocide, racial hatred or misogyny infect certain nations." He rubbed his chin. "So, what would America's persona be?"

She shrugged her shoulders. "Maybe she's the sum of all the individual lives in her past and present. Their actions, stemming from their values and beliefs, created and continue to create karmas. Maybe all these individual karmas, put together, form not only her personality but also chart her future. In that sense, she is very much alive."

"America's karma, right?"

"Of course."

Sam whistled. "Wow! That's way too deep for me!" He turned his attention to the map. "Look. Here's Boulder," he said. "And Denver's here. My Ma and Grandma live there."

She touched the spot with her finger. "How about your father?"

Sam frowned. "I haven't seen my father since I was little."

Chantley's eyes widened. Sam looked angry. So different from her relationship with her father! "Your family's been here for a while?"

"Yes. In the early 1900s, my great-grandfather moved here from back east, bought some land near Greeley and started a ranch."

"Back east?"

"My grandma said our ancestors came to America as slaves in the early 1800s." He pointed to a patch of land in the southeast corner of the continent. "They worked on a plantation in South Carolina." He followed the coast with his finger and stopped upon reaching Baltimore, situated at the north end of an enormous bay. "In the 1850s, before the civil war, they escaped and settled there." Chantley rubbed her chin, trying to remember. Didn't someone from the ashram move to that area? The name escaped her.

"I may still have relations in Baltimore," he continued, "but since my great-grandfather's time, we've lost track of them."

He pointed to another spot. Pittsburgh. She hesitantly moved her finger eastwards from Denver until it landed on that city. The distance frightened her. It seemed half a world away. Did she have the courage to board a bus and travel there by herself? How many days would it take? What would she do upon arrival? She gulped, imagining herself stepping off the bus in an unknown city with no one to greet her.

Sam interrupted her thoughts. "I just realized something!"

"What's that?"

"You've become disconnected from your roots just like I have!"

She nodded her head. Sam was right, of course. Did something pull her back to this country, something much larger and more mysterious than the obvious ones of broken relationships and loss of loved ones? We all think we act according to an unbroken line of deed and result, but do we have the intelligence to discern what is cause and what is consequence? Or are actions and reactions so subtly stretched over time that we're barely cognizant of them?

Chantley recreated the story of Sam's ancestry in her mind. His story differed so much from hers! A doubt arose. Maybe they shared no karmic connection. She gazed wistfully at him. Sooner or later, she would leave Boulder. Perhaps, the whole thing will end before it even starts—another dead end. But still, the question of shared past lives gnawed at her.

Sam closed the atlas and looked up. "I saw my mom and grandma last night," he announced.

"That's nice," she said, nodding her head abstractedly.

"I mentioned you to them."

She looked at him wide-eyed. Aren't we just acquaintances? I hope he said nothing more than that. "What did they say?"

"They were real curious. Especially with you being raised in India and..."

"And what?" she prodded.

Sam cleared his throat. "And you being white."

Chantley's mind went blank. Did they approve?

"It surprised them." He laughed. "I'm surprised myself."

She shot him a quizzical look.

"Most of my friends are black," he explained. "Besides, I never had any white female friends."

Friends. For the first time, Sam defined their relationship. A twinge of hurt emerged, but she instantly shook it off. Sam was right: they were friends, nothing more. "Why didn't you?" she asked.

Sam whistled. "It's a long story. My grandma married a white man. Then, one day, he just left her. It devastated my family."

Chantley's eyes widened. Is this the end? She steadied herself. "What did they ask about me?"

"Just my interest in you."

Chantley's eyes sharpened, and her heart pounded.

"I told them that maybe we knew each other from a previous life!" Sam laughed. "They thought it was weird."

Chantley gasped. "And what do you think?"

He shrugged his shoulders. "Who knows? I don't pay much attention to that kind of stuff. I'm not so spiritual. I'm more interested in what's going on in this world."

She puckered her lips and looked at him with disappointment.

"You believe that stuff, don't you?" he asked.

She looked away. *Should I press this further*, she wondered. She opened her mouth to affirm her position but closed it. *Now is not the right time. I don't want to give the impression that I want to be anything more than just a friend.*

"I'd like to know." She shrugged her shoulders. "But it's just curiosity." She forced a smile. "What else did you talk about?"

"My Grandma asked me how we got along so well so quickly."

"Really?"

"Yeah. I kind of wonder about that myself." He looked at her. "It's never happened before. It usually takes me a long time to connect with people, especially women."

Chantley understood his character by now. Fiercely intellectual and brilliantly creative. The kind who understands the world mostly with his mind but not enough with his heart. Devours books but doesn't listen to his intuition. Full of passionate argument and debate but not soft understanding. She stopped. *I'm being too hard on Sam. He has strong opinions, but he's charming and immensely helpful. Who else has shown me such consideration?*

Besides, she understood her character diametrically opposed to his. She remained shy, retiring and intuitive. Intellectual too, but in a different sort of way. Yes, she attended college, but overall, its impact on her was minimal: her experiences at the ashram defined her way of thinking. *We are different*, she decided. *That might be the secret: not only do we attract but also balance each other.*

Chapter Ten

Their first kiss occurred mid-afternoon, under the shade of a maple tree, in the center of the main quad on Campus. They stopped at the end of a long walk through Boulder after coffee and dessert downtown. The early summer brought a fierce heat that left Chantley's arms red and her face tender, and they rested under the tree for relief, not romance. She ran her hands against its dark trunk and looked up. The branches sprouted new leaves, some just-born, others full size, as sap flowed up the trunk after the long coldness of winter.

She stood silently under the shade, brushing up against Sam, waiting for the heat to escape her clothes and her skin to cool. She closed her eyes, hearing only the breeze murmuring among the leaves while it freshened her body. The moment felt perfect—the long walk had induced contemplation, her legs were pleasantly tired, the cooling shade supplied satisfaction, and his companionship grounded her spirit. She emptied her mind and reveled in the quiet.

After a while, she opened her eyes, feeling something amiss. Sam's total silence was unlike him. She looked at him questioningly, and he stared back awkwardly, hesitantly. He moved closer and rubbed his hands up her still-warm arms and shoulders. His face moved just inches in front of hers.

Suddenly, he snatched her close and kissed her. Chantley's heart fluttered like a captured bird, both in fear of being ensnared and in the excitement of surrender. She shook like a leaf, and the hair on her arms and neck stood up. Sam tightened his embrace. She capitulated, closed her eyes and allowed an aching sweetness to enter.

In a moment, it was over. But something had changed. Chantley's chest heaved and the blood drained from her face. Sam brought out something from deep within; it both frightened and excited her.

She and Vijay had been virgin lovers. It was pure, achingly so, as they stole kisses, held hands, looked into each other's eyes, planned their futures and dreamt of endless bliss in each other's arms. But nothing she did with Vijay agitated her, overpowered her, like this. Her heart wanted to shout out eternal love, but her mind stopped her cold. It was exactly what she desired but also precisely what she hoped to avoid.

"That was nice," he said.

Chantley's mind spun. She had traveled out of her body, rocketed to the planets, spun among the stars and hurtled frighteningly back to earth, all in a few seconds. And all Sam had to say was, 'nice?'

Her eyes widened, but she controlled her wonder. "Yes, it was."

Sam nodded his head triumphantly.

*****

Chantley came down from her room for breakfast the following day and stumbled upon Charles sitting at the kitchen island.

"Oh," she remarked. "I didn't expect you to be here."

"I thought I'd join you for breakfast today." He pointed to the seat to his right. "Sit down, and I'll prepare everything."

"That's okay," she objected. "I'll get the toast and jam. I know where it is."

"No," he commanded. "Today, I'll serve you." He got up, opened the fridge door, retrieved the bread, butter, and jam, prepared the toast, poured a glass of orange juice, and presented it to her.

"Thank you," she said, slightly non-plussed by the attention.

"You're welcome," he replied, sitting next to her.

They talked about the ashram, her friendship with Candace and her plans.

Charles reached out and held Chantley's left hand. At that moment, Candace entered the kitchen. Chantley turned red and snapped her hand back. Her friend stared at them, poured herself a cup of coffee, and quickly left.

"I have to leave," Chantley mumbled.

Chapter Eleven

Chantley met Sam at the University. The place proved busy: students lay sprawled on the grass studying, others tossed Frisbees, while professors in jackets strolled the sidewalks. They sat under a large tree on the west side of the quad, near the library, where the late morning sun shone. Chantley crossed her feet and tucked the edges of her calf-length, cream-colored skirt under her knees. She paired it with a printed rose-red, short-sleeved, cotton blouse while a large crimson satin flower lay pinned in her hair. The ensemble had a distinct fifties look, but her fresh frame and appealing face breathed new life into old fashion. Sam wore a light-blue denim shirt, sleeves rolled up, and navy-blue jeans with a brown braided cloth belt. He didn't have his hat, and his hair was cut short.

Three weeks of near-constant meetings—lunches, afternoon-long walks, sittings on park benches watching children play and extended excursions into curio shops—had passed. Despite her rationalizations, Chantley felt her heart open up to Sam. Her chest tightened, and every time they met, the feeling strengthened, and his emotional contours—the meaning of a smile, whether ironic, appreciative or bemused—became clearer. Her face—the pursing of her lips, the arch of her eyebrows and the tightening of her cheeks—reflected her feelings.

The effortlessness of their friendship and the natural deepening of their bond suggested an intimacy beyond the bounds of this life. How else could she explain the ease with which she recognized the emotional signposts, pitfalls, and detours? Sam needed to be made aware of this. But, like a secret kept from a close friend, it would only be a matter of time before being revealed. She maintained patience.

"That's it!" he exclaimed.

"What?"

"My last exam."

"How did you do?"

Sam laughed, his eyes gleaming, the skin forming wrinkles at their edges. "I'm sure I did well."

"What course was that?"

"Sociology and Slavery," he replied.

"What's it about?"

Sam creased his eyebrows. "The important point is this: if you look at what we go through today, such as poverty, violence and injustice, it all goes back to slave times."

"Colonization had similar effects in India," she responded. "Things like scarcity, lack of opportunity and Indians' alienation from their history and spiritual heritage."

"You're comparing slavery with colonization?"

The discussion reminded her of similar ones back at the Women's College. She perked up. "Yes. Classical colonization is the control of not just the political and economic institutions by a conquering one but also the cultural and religious imposition of a subject people. Slavery and colonization occurred at the same time. Slavery is colonization taken to an extreme."

"That's an interesting statement!" Sam paused. "But it's not the same thing. India was colonized but never enslaved. Fanon said that white society smashed the old world of the African without giving him a new one. Slavery blocked the road to the future after having closed the road of the past. As V.S. Naipaul wrote, India may be a wounded civilization, but it has survived."

His rejoinder stumped her. She had read about American racism at the Women's College, but it always confounded her. "Why is there racism against black people?" she asked perfectly reasonably.

Sam's jaw dropped. "What did you say?"

"Why is there a racist attitude toward black people in America?" she repeated matter-of-factly.

Sam eyed her incredulously and burst out laughing. "You're serious, aren't you?"

Chantley squirmed. Am I being gauche? Does he think of me as being stupid? She looked away with a hint of desperation in her eyes.

"You don't know anything about this country, do you?"

She wriggled a bit more. "No, I don't," she admitted, her voice reflecting her hesitancy.

Sam shook his head. "No one's asked me that question quite that way. I've thought about it for years. But I suppose the answer is quite simple."

Chantley looked at him expectantly.

"See, it has to do with power. When the two races first met, one had all the power, and the other didn't. Therefore, one became exploited, and the other the exploiter. Once the relationship was established, all sorts of explanations and dissimulations were created to mask its immorality."

"Like what?"

"That the exploited deserve to be exploited. Because it's meant to be this way. Put in any adjective you want: lazy, irresponsible or genetically inferior. Racism is nothing more than the artificial justification for the master-slave relationship; that is, blaming the victim for his or her condition. It's a mechanism by which the powerful deny and validate the situation for their benefit."

Chantley considered Sam's reply. It was perfectly true; depressingly so. And his exposition explained its prevalence, to one degree or another, in all societies. In India, that powerful-powerless equation manifested in Dalit, sometimes called Untouchable, relationships. In the Middle East, racism expressed itself in religious terms; in Africa, of dominant tribes versus weaker ones; and in the West, based on color. By Sam's description, racism probably existed in every human society since time immemorial.

"Let me put it to you this way," continued Sam. "If blacks had as much power when the races first interacted, there would have been no racism. It's got nothing to do with color. Racism is a function of unequal relationships."

Chantley immediately had an idea. "So, if black-white relationships can be re-established in America based on equality, then racism can be solved!" she stated brightly.

Sam doubled up in laughter.

Chantley's forehead wrinkled. Didn't I honestly address the problem at its root? "What?" she asked self-consciously.

"If only it could be solved so easily! Look, this is not a theoretical question. It's real."

"Doesn't what I say make sense?"

"It does," agreed Sam. "In a charming, though naïve, kind of way. I have no idea how, if at all, you can re-establish race relations in this country after everything that has happened. In fact, I don't think it's possible."

His answer stumped Chantley. She had to admit her ignorance of the culture and her answers to be, maybe, simplistic. She looked at Sam and suddenly realized that, with her white skin, a gulf existed between them. By living among Indians, having Indian friends and speaking their language, her self-image was that of an Indian girl. She had found comfort and familiarity with Sam's dark skin. Now the discussion brought out the stark difference. She felt insecure. Would this dissimilarity build an invisible wall between them? he dearly wished not. She needed Sam. Another thought arose. Sam's rootedness in this place contrasted ironically with her rootlessness. Despite the history of alienation he described, it remained his history, whereas she searched for hers.

"I like you," exclaimed Sam. "I've never met anyone like you."

Chantley let go of her anxiety and smiled.

*****

The announcement fell like a bombshell. As Charles gawked at Chantley, Candace spoke with knotted eyebrows. "I'll be traveling to Belize for the next month. You'll have to find another place. You can take a couple of days."

Stunned, Chantley nodded her head numbly.

"You can move in with me," offered Sam the next day, over coffee at the Mall in Boulder.

Chantley's eyes bulged. Move in with a man! She had heard stories of Americans living together without ever getting married. Or even having children out of wedlock. She shook her head. She could never do that.

"I'm sorry," she mumbled. "I've never lived with a man."

Sam's scratched his head. "I sense something else. How old are you?"

"Twenty-one."

Sam stared at her for several long seconds. "Have you ever been with a man?"

She instantly turned crimson. What could be the reason for such a question? What does he think of me? Deeply embarrassed, she kept her gaze on the ground while silently shaking her head.

"Whooeee!" He whistled in surprise. He got up and walked back and forth. "I've got to say, that's different. I mean, if you can do that, well, hats off to you."

Chantley relaxed.

Sam shook his head. "I can't believe how sheltered you are. I got to warn you, America is not at all like how you grew up. It can eat up women like you in no time flat. In middle school, girls, thirteen years old, came to classes with swollen bellies." He looked into her eyes. "I don't know how long you're going to last here with those values."

She shrugged her shoulders. "That's the way I was raised."

"You are so unusual! I can't believe it!"

She beamed, immensely thankful for his understanding, for not pressing her. "Thanks."

Sam helped her find the most economical hostel in Boulder. He bought her a cell phone, something cheap but convenient, to keep in touch. She paid for the plan.

Chapter Twelve

So that's it! She's inexperienced with men, and that's why she blows hot and cold. Sam understood it to be cultural; most countries didn't share America's views on sexuality. The Chinese and Arabs, not to mention Indians, differed sharply from the West on this topic. He rubbed his chin. Even in Western countries, before the sexual revolution of the 1960s, sexual mores were much more conservative. Despite his surprise at her position, he understood its origins.

He felt like a diver who finds a rare pearl in the middle of the ocean. Chantley was undoubtedly a jewel, one in a million. He felt ever more protective of her. *I have to make sure she makes the right choices; that no harm comes to her.* Others would take advantage of such a young woman's naiveté. *How should I react to this? She was too innocent to be pressed: she might react badly. I'll wait as long as I have to. After all, this was proving to be a special relationship.*

Yet, he felt alarm. She's twenty-one, but a young twenty-one. Her sheltered life in the ashram couldn't have prepared her for the world's financial, cultural, or interpersonal challenges. He shook his head, sensing what she was up against. At least I have my Grandma and my Ma, whereas she's lost everyone. No wonder she seemed fragile and sensitive. *Does she realize what she's up against?*

Sam wrapped the raincoat tightly around his body and adjusted the hat on his head. The rain lashed the skyscrapers, streamed down the glass windows, flooded the black pavement and poured into the storm drains. He looked around. The restaurants and bars stayed tightly shut as he walked, block after block, down the deserted streets, his footsteps echoing on the pavement. The early Sunday morning forced solitude upon the city. He enjoyed it. It suited him to be alone with his thoughts.

He had left Boulder early in the morning to visit his family but, at the last moment, took the exit to downtown Denver. Yesterday, Ma and Grandma had joined him at the graduation ceremony. There were hugs, congratulations, and dinner at an expensive restaurant. He finally had his degree in his pocket. He should be thrilled, but instead, Sam felt vacant. With what did he end up? A piece of paper and not much else.

After four years on campus, how would he handle living with family again? Being forced out of the dorm to return home felt like a defeat. He would be back where he started. He didn't mind Ma, but Grandma would get on his nerves. She would pressure him to make money. He weighed his options. He could go to graduate school, but he had studied as much as he wanted. He could find work, but no career felt appealing.

Sam walked glumly back to the car. He wasn't in the mood to start the conversation with his Grandma about returning home. Instead, he'd wait until the last minute until he had no choice.

*****

Chantley walked by the side of Boulder Creek and watched the waters race away as raindrops fell through the dense mist darkening the day. She had awoken at the break of dawn, when the barest of glimmers peeked over the mountains, and walked through the hardly-stirring town. Her stroll had taken her from the hostel's front steps, through the town's exclusive neighborhoods, on moist pavements, past lush lawns and wet rose gardens, under dripping elm trees and into the park not far from downtown. She bundled the thin coat tightly around herself, tightened the scarf around her neck and listened to the irregular drumbeat of raindrops bouncing off the top of her black umbrella.

The soft gray clamshell of low clouds and high ground created both a mood of contemplation and a sense of mute insulation, drowning out all distractions while freeing her mind. After weeks of constant companionship, she relished being alone with her thoughts.

She stopped at a spot where several large flat rocks bordered the creek. The melting snows from the mountains engorged the stream, and the dark green water splashed, gurgled and bubbled swiftly past her. Hidden under her large umbrella, she hunched on the riverbank and threw a pebble in the water. It bounced once, then settled to the bottom.

A family of ducks, the mother with sleek brown feathers, a flat yellow beak and three fluffy, yellow-brown, cotton-ball ducklings possessing tiny bright-black eyes, waddled right up to the water on the other side of the creek. The mother assessed the terrain, taking several steps one way and another, possibly seeking a safe entrance to the water. The duck quacked softly as she strode, her brood scrambling willy-nilly behind her on toothpick legs. Chantley regarded them with alarm; the waters seemed too dangerous to cross. After a couple of minutes, they disappeared into the bushes lining the banks, and Chantley reverted to her reverie.

The episode with Candace chilled her like a cold shower. The free room, not to mention Sam's attention, had buffered her and helped her avoid making a decision. Now, everything became clear: she had to leave Boulder as soon as possible. Despite the hostel being the cheapest accommodation available, it was becoming an unbearable expense.

Why did I stay here so long? The answer came quickly: Sam. She pursed her lips. Who is Sam? Someone she met just a month ago. But he had only been a distraction from her mission. He couldn't do anything to settle her future. Her mother remained the only hope for securing her prospects. So far, her American experience had been a prelude. Her mother would be the actual starting point. She shrugged her shoulders. Her friendship with Sam wasn't the only reason for the delay. She hadn't the courage to make the journey.

What am I going to tell Sam? I don't want to hurt him, but I have no choice. I wish it had been different. She stopped. *Why am I feeling this way? Isn't he just a friend? Isn't that what he said?*

Immediately, like an itch too long ignored, the thought of their karmic past re-surfaced. *Is this why I haven't moved on?* That mystery, the bond she felt afraid to question Sam about, the one she insisted on pushing into the recesses of her mind, unsettled her once again. Her heart struggled with nervous energy. *I could ask him about it, but most likely, I will have to let the question go unanswered.* She grimaced, her mouth turning down. And let it bother me for the rest of my life.

Suddenly, the family of ducks burst noisily into the scene right next to her. Chantley raised the umbrella's brow and stared right into the mother's eyes. With her beak partially open, the duck stared at her sheepishly, almost apologetically, for the rude interruption. The little ones observed the comical standoff in absolute silence, their unblinking eyes darting from one party to the other. Chantley arched her eyebrows. How did they cross the creek? She looked at the spot where she saw them last. The waterway curved and disappeared. Did they discover a bridge of stones connecting the two shores further downstream? Or did the creek widen and thus slow down sufficiently to swim across? Whatever the case, the mother duck had found the courage to cross over.

The mother duck immediately turned around, wagged her feathered behind a couple of times, and quickly retreated under the bushes from where she had come as her brood ran maniacally behind, emitting high-pitched chirps.

Chantley stood up, her heart filling with resolve. *It's time. The next chance I get, I'll inform Sam of my plans to move on.*

Chapter Thirteen

The following Saturday, Sam asked Chantley to accompany him on a hike to Boulder Canyon with several of his friends. She looked at him in alarm.

"I've always been alone with you," she remarked. "I've never pictured you as part of a bigger crowd."

Sam laughed. "I have friends. Always have."

"What will they say about me?"

"Don't worry. They'll like you."

"What will they talk about?" She looked at him in alarm. "What will I wear?"

"Okay, don't worry," Sam said, "I'll buy you an outfit."

"You don't have to," she protested.

"I insist," replied Sam gallantly.

They visited a small shop three blocks off the Mall, where the prices looked more reasonable. He pulled a small black dress, matched with a smart white blouse, off the rack. Chantley laughed.

"What?" he asked.

"I can't wear this!"

Sam rubbed his forehead. "Why not?"

"That's ridiculous! How can I go for a hike wearing that little thing?"

The search for a suitable outfit took most of the afternoon.

"Now I remember why I hated shopping with my mother," he finally exclaimed.

"There," said Chantley pointing to a Nepali import store. Ten minutes later, they marched out with a white baggy harem pant, which she called a Punjabi, a short-sleeved, thigh-long, beige blouse paired with a light-cream cotton shawl.

"This looks like another piece of your Indian clothes!"

"Yes," she replied. "Isn't it nice?"

Sam laughed and rolled his eyes in humor. "All right. Let's get this party started."

The heat in the valley transformed into a soft white flannel blanket floating halfway up the hills, while above, the red setting sun colored the cirrus clouds in the turquoise sky. The thin black road flowed along the canyon's bottom while a series of huge flat red rocks, resembling scales on dinosaurs' backs, climbed up the hillsides, jutting perpendicularly into the sky.

They met six others—a white couple and four single black men—in the parking lot for a post-graduation get-together. After this, the dorm rooms would clear out, and the seniors would return home or escape to jobs in parts unknown.

He introduced her to DeAngelo, who was tall, clean-shaven and well-dressed. "This is my roommate."

He gazed at her with interest. "Sam mentioned you a couple of times."

Chantley drew surprised glances from the others. She blushed. Sam understood her thoughts. It's because we are an interracial couple.

They found a trail and started climbing. Sweet-smelling red dirt, fragrant spruce and the tang of the pine trees filled the air. Sam breathed deeply. The natural surroundings invigorated him, and the trek brought a spring to his steps. The thin mile-high air heated rapidly during the day and, just as quickly, cooled in the evenings. At dusk, the temperature felt perfect, and a soft wind caressed his face.

After an hour, upon reaching the top of the hill, they discovered a tiny, deserted picnic area featuring a fire pit. One of the men produced a boom-box while Sam and the others sat in a circle around the small bonfire. Chantley perched herself just behind Sam. Someone opened a backpack and brought out beer. Sam took one and offered her another.

"No thanks," replied Chantley and moved further back.

The friends started talking, mostly about their university experiences and prospects.

"You guys are all smart," declared Sam. "I should have known better. A major in American History doesn't open many doors."

"There's no reason why you shouldn't find a job," said John hopefully, who, along with Carla, formed the white couple. "You're one of the smartest guys I know."

'I don't know." Sam sighed. "I think something else is going on here."

"What?" asked DeAngelo.

Sam straightened up. "Do you all mind if I ask a question?" They nodded their heads.

"Anyone who has a job, raise your hand."

DeAngelo raised his hand. "I got a six-month engineering internship."

John and Carla also raised their hands. Fortunately, both were offered full-time jobs. "I don't know," said Carla reassuringly, "it's just a bad economy out there."

Sam's eyes shone. "No," he asserted. "It's more than that. Look at the statistics. Unemployment rates among blacks are always higher than whites, and it doesn't matter what age and education levels are. It's always been like that."

The black men nodded their heads understandingly. John and Carla squirmed.

"Look, it's not about you," Sam continued, addressing the couple. "I love you guys. And it's not about anyone else. It's the system. It's broken. There's an institutional bias that treats black people different and, despite so many efforts for change, it's still not working."

"We need to change the system," replied DeAngelo.

Sam pushed his glasses up his nose and vigorously jabbed his finger in the air. "But isn't that what we've been trying for the last fifty years? Martin Luther King and all that? Things have got better, I'll admit, but are we happy with where we are?" His eyes blazed. "Is this justice?"

They all shook their heads. Sam looked around. The others were used to his pontificating, but he noticed Chantley's raised eyebrows.

"What's the alternative?" asked DeAngelo.

"According to W.E.B. DuBois, we should create our businesses and communities and generate jobs. We can't wait for the government to change things." Sam hesitated a few seconds. Others had proposed much more radical solutions. Frantz Fanon believed only a violent revolution could change things. He argued that decolonization was a violent process and halfway methods only allowed unjust institutions and attitudes to survive. A very seductive idea, it found resonance in America. "And Malcolm X," he continued, "said that we are a separate nation, that blacks should have their own country in America."

John and Carla squirmed some more.

"It all goes back to slavery," he stated. "We think that slavery is dead, and our economic and political system has moved on." He looked at his friends closely and continued eagerly. "But if you look at much of what we go through—broken families, poverty, lack of education and jobs—it can be traced, in one way or another, back to slavery."

DeAngelo smiled. "Man, you're always talking about slavery. Why are you so interested in it?"

Sam reflected. "I feel like a bit of my soul is there with those slaves. If we could go back, we would understand who we are and how we got here."

"Whoa. That's deep!" exclaimed DeAngelo. They all laughed. "Hey man," he continued, "let's just have some fun."

Sam laughed, slapped his friend's hand, and sat down. They talked, the alcohol loosening their tongues, their conversations becoming more animated, their expressions getting extravagant, and the music playing louder. After a while, he looked behind him and saw Chantley gazing off in the distance. She had kept to herself all the time.

"Are you having fun?" he asked. She smiled and nodded her head. He hugged her. "Good. I knew you would."

Finally, the party started petering out. Sam's friends stretched out on the ground, not conversing.

Chantley tugged Sam's shirt. "Let's go."

"But everyone's still here," he countered.

"It's been a long evening," she whispered.

Sam pushed his glasses up his nose. "You've been very quiet."

Chantley let out a long-suppressed sigh of frustration. "What am I supposed to do? I don't know anyone."

He pulled her over. "I'm sorry. Let's get out of here."

Sam shook his friends' hands, said goodbyes and made promises to keep in touch. He held Chantley's hand as they walked back down. The moon glowed huge and yellow, illuminating the white birches and red boulders and turning a spotlight on the valley below. It sparkled over the liquid silver band of the highway snaking out of the canyon and, further beyond, behind high hills, competed with the glow of the city spread out on the plains.

"Let's spend some time here," volunteered Chantley at a hill crest. They found two tall evergreens and sat across from each other at their bases, the moonlight streaming on their faces.

Sam stared at her and whistled.

"What are you thinking?" she asked.

"That you're the prettiest girl I ever met!'

She laughed for a moment and then turned serious. "I'll be leaving in a couple of days." She looked down. "I'm sorry. I appreciate everything you've done, but I've run out of options. I can't stay in Boulder any longer."

Sam kept quiet for some time. He had expected this after she had to move out of her friend's house, but it still stung. "Where will you be going?" he asked.

"Pittsburgh. To look for my mother."

"Well, good luck." He looked away. His delivery had been too straight, and his voice revealed a touch of reticence, a hint of hurt.

"I'm sorry," she repeated. "You've been my anchor, helping steady me when I didn't know what would happen."

He nodded his head. A deep bond had formed, revealing itself now upon saying their goodbyes.

"It's okay," he answered, "you've got to do what you have to."

"Maybe we can keep in touch?" she suggested.

Sam breathed deeply and shook his head. "I appreciate that, but sometimes it's better to let things end. We've had fun, and I enjoyed being with you. You're unlike anyone I've ever met. You have to go, and I'm a free bird right now. I don't have a job and don't know where I'm going."

She looked up at the stars now shining in the sky. "Do you remember what I said when we first met?" she asked.

"What's that?'

"I'm unsure how to say this," she mumbled, "but I have a strong feeling that I know you from before, maybe from a previous life."

"I remember you telling me." He gazed at her. "You really believe this stuff, don't you?"

She nodded her head.

"I get it. You were raised in that culture. It's the way you think."

"It's more than that."

"What do you mean?"

"It's about us. We're saying our goodbyes, but it will gnaw at me for a long time if I don't figure out what it means. Sorting it out will allow me to move on. But," she quickly added, "it's up to you."

"How do you figure out what happened in previous lives?"

"In India, people consult a Vedic astrologer to see what samskaras, that is, patterns from the past, are carried over."

Sam laughed. "I don't think you will find any genuine Vedic astrologers around here."

Chantley's eyes dropped, crestfallen.

"But there is a new-age journal here in Boulder that carries ads for past-life regressions. I can look it up tomorrow."

"Really?"

"Sure. If it makes you happy."

She hesitated. "You don't have to."

It was the least he could do. "It's my parting gift!"

Chapter Fourteen

Dr. Carmen Dwyer, a petite woman in her late thirties, displayed her name and credentials—B.Sc., M.Sc., Ph.D. (Psychology), Certified Clinical Hypnotherapist—on a framed parchment on the receptionist's desk in a nondescript office in a strip-mall off Baseline Street. She wore a gray business suit, cut stylishly to fit her slim frame, and tied her medium-length, dark-brown hair tightly behind her head with a red ribbon. She peered at Chantley and Sam over horn-rimmed glasses perched on the brow of her nose.

"Who am I speaking to?"

"Sam. Sam DeVon Johnson," he replied, "and this is Chantley Armstrong."

The doctor's unexpectedly firm handshake surprised her.

"We're here to talk about a past-life regression," he said hesitantly.

Dr. Dwyer nodded her head. "Yes, we do that."

Sam looked around. "I wasn't expecting this."

She smiled as if she knew what was coming. "What did you expect?"

"Someone with a crystal ball and incense floating in the air."

"I use hypnotherapy in past-life regressions," she informed him. "Hypnotherapy has been recognized as a valid medical procedure by American Medical Association since 1958."

"You're saying hypnotherapy will take us back to previous lives?"

"As I'm sure you understand, reincarnation, which is tied in with past-life regression, is not accepted as a scientific fact. In hypnotherapy, I don't lead you to any conclusions. I only act as a guide and interpreter, but you are the one who drives the car, as it were. You are always in control."

"Then explain to me how this works."

"When we meet a person for the first time, or when something new happens, we experience it in different ways; physically, emotionally and mentally. These original reactions are stored as memories. Those same reactions are triggered upon meeting that person again or a similar event occurring. These may be positive or negative, but they repeatedly happen until a pattern forms. In Regression Therapy, the trained therapist guides you to remember that original event."

Chantley nodded her head. She understood the doctor's explanation, even if couched in scientific jargon. If she substituted the word karma for the initial reaction and samskaras for the subtle physical, mental and emotional patterns, it didn't differ from what she had learned. And instead of certified therapists, trained spiritual guides, such as swamis or pundits, led the explorations.

"So, what do you do?" Sam asked Dr. Dwyer.

"Based on your goal, I will ask you questions and guide the session."

"That's it?"

"That's it." She laughed. "But the devil is in the details. Like a skilled teacher or a capable coach, a good therapist can be invaluable."

"What will happen during this session?"

"We have a saying that all hypnosis is self-hypnosis—that is, I will give you suggestions, and it is up to you to follow them. I will guide you in relaxation until you reach what we call a 'passive state,' where you'll be able to access hidden memories and deep, subtle impressions."

Sam took a deep breath. "Wow!"

She picked up a clipboard holding some forms and led them down a hallway into a darkened room with a reclining chair. "Who's doing the therapy?"

Sam raised his hand.

"Go ahead and sit down."

Sam climbed into the chair and relaxed while the doctor sat on a chair to his right side.

"Does this concern her?" Dr. Dwyer asked, glancing at Chantley. Sam nodded his head.

"She can stay here only with your permission," she replied, tapping her pen lightly on the clipboard.

"Sure," replied Sam. "She has my permission."

"When doing a single regression, I like to be alone with the client. However, in this case, your friend can stay as long as she remains in the background and keeps quiet."

Chantley wagged her head and moved to the shadows near the door, well behind Sam.

"What's going on?" asked Dr. Dwyer.

"Chantley feels that we have a connection from a previous life."

The doctor removed her glasses and placed them on a small table. "Okay. Our goal will be to determine if you had a previous soul connection and to determine its nature," she stated, writing it down on a form on the clipboard.

Chantley reflected. The doctor brought it out so directly and so neatly. In her experience, it involved so much more: the feelings raised, the physicality of the relationship, the promises made to each other, the obligations expected and even the spiritual aspects—a woman's point of view. Yet this doctor seemed comfortable with her presentation as if her profession demanded deconstruction.

"Close your eyes," said the doctor. Though directed at Sam, Chantley automatically closed her eyes as well.

"Inhale deeply."

Chantley took several long, deep breaths, raising and lowering her diaphragm, letting the calmness spread through her body.

"Now relax your fingers. Let them fall." The loosening of the arms, facial muscles, legs and feet followed. After many minutes, she introduced imagery.

"Take your mind to a calm and relaxed place. Maybe a country setting?"

Chantley recognized the breath control and the use of imagery as meditational techniques she had taught at the ashram. The mood in the small dark room acquired a spiritual flavor. She felt herself enter the stillness, the meditative silence that hung in the air, sliding down a well-known path, partaking of the session in her own manner and, in some ways, accessing Sam's thoughts as he delved into his consciousness.

She slowly immersed herself into Sam's psyche, slipping into his character without even trying, like a child who understands communication through pure emotions, before words and objects came between thoughts and meanings. She felt others' joys and disappointments, and her face reflected their moods purely. But it had proven to be a double-edged sword. Her perceptiveness left her vulnerable to hurt and disappointment. Her friends had told her that she was too sensitive.

Finally, the doctor softly counted down from ten. Chantley, observing Sam's hands on the armrests, understood by their complete relaxation that he had arrived at the passive state.

"Can you picture your friend now?' asked the therapist.

"Yes," he replied.

"Can you describe her?"

"She has long, pretty fingers."

Chantley flushed. What a strange thing to notice!

"What else?"

"I felt deeply connected to her the first time we met."

Her intuition had been correct! She beamed, feeling his warm smile through the dark.

"When I first saw her, I sensed a strange awkwardness, as if not knowing what to say. I'm kind of surprised we got along so well, so quickly."

"Anything else?"

"With her, there's no judgment. She treats me like I'm just another human being, and in the beginning, it felt a bit unnerving."

Chantley stood still in the dark, cheeks red, warmth enveloping her.

"Good! Now let's see where you met previously." Dr. Dwyer patiently took Sam back, one question at a time, one suggestion after another, through the haze of time and the mist of years until he had a breakthrough.

"Where are you now?"

Sam spoke through a hypnotic haze. "I'm standing at the entrance to a large room."

"Describe it."

"Across from me are several large windows. A huge four-post bed with an enormous trunk in front is pushed up against the right wall. On the left is a big oval mirror in a carved wood frame resembling a climbing rose bush with small buds at its edges. Several paintings of men and women in formal poses and dressed in antique clothes hang on the pale-green walls. The ceiling is quite high, crossed by thick red wooden beams. A crystal chandelier, with several wax candles, hangs from its center."

"Keep going."

"Now I'm walking to the windows directly across me. I swing one open and look out. It's late afternoon, and the weather's warm."

"Describe the place."

"The mansion is set in a large estate. In front, four carriages with horses are waiting on a circular-shaped driveway. A sandy road, three hundred feet long, lined on both sides with oak trees, starts from the circular driveway, travels through the lawn, past gardens of rose bushes—red, yellow and orange—and ends at a solid wooden gate set in a brick wall. On the other side of the gate is the main street. Rows of tall green bushes with short leaves run along the walls on each side of the house. I smell jasmine—sweet and strong."

"Go ahead," she said in a low, measured, professional voice.

"On both sides of the property, I see fields. They're growing some grain—not wheat—maybe rice. The plants are set in fields covered with water. In front, across the street, is another field looking like an impenetrable jungle. It's sugarcane, I think. The stalks are taller than a man, with long thin leaves on top."

"Can you see anything else?"

A long silence ensued. "If I stick my head out of the window and turn it to the right, I see a dozen small and square buildings along the side wall. The closest ones are built with brown bricks, chimneys, and dark slate roofs. Some have doors, and some do not. Further down are others, long and narrow with wooden frames, like army barracks. The ground in front of the buildings is muddy."

"Do you see any people?"

"A few, in the close-by brick houses. The others are empty. Maybe they are out working."

"Do you see any signs or markings?"

Chantley imagined Sam surveying the scene, looking for letters or symbols.

"Above the gate in front of the house are two curved black metal arches, parallel to each other. And between the arches are metal letters."

Chantley felt Sam leaning out the window, his hands clasping the sill, straining to read the lettering. Did this scene, the roses, the walls, the fields and the house feel familiar to her? She examined her heart but got nothing.

He spelled out the letters: C,O, O, P, E, R and then, R, I, V, E,R. A short pause ensued. "It reads 'Cooper River Plantation, Charleston.'" Sam's arms straightened. "Oh my God! This is a slave plantation! I can't believe it. I'm a slave, and I'm looking out of the master's bedroom!" Sam's breathing quickened. Chantley's heart beat faster.

"Calm down," instructed the doctor, and after a few seconds, she asked, "How do you feel about where you are?"

"Strange," he replied, his breathing still restless. "I know it's home, but I feel a sense of dread. I've lived here all my life, but I must leave."

His breathing became more agitated. "I don't see anything now. I've lost the connection."

Dr. Dwyer replaced the glasses on her nose. "Relax. Keep breathing," she said softly, yet with authority. Sam slowly calmed down. Chantley closed her eyes and pacified her heartbeat. After the doctor became convinced of his readiness, she restarted the process. "Go back to where you were."

He connected to the scene again. "It's now dark, though a bit of light remains. It's probably seven or seven-thirty in the evening. From the slave quarters, I hear many muffled voices, but inside the house, it's absolutely silent, like everyone has left. I hear crickets in the grass and frogs croaking from the fields." A pause ensued. "Something's happening!"

"What?"

"A group of black men are emerging from the tall sugarcane across the road. They have weapons—long staves and even rifles. There must be thirty, forty, of them, mostly young. A few are just children. Most have no shoes. They're dressed in raggedy clothing, torn shirts and patched pants, but some have gray coats and caps. Wait, they've crossed the road, and they're trying to smash down the gate!"

"What else?"

"Slaves are running out of their homes and towards the gate! It's my chance to escape. I jump up and run out of the bedroom room. On the way out, I see a rifle near the door. I grab it. Now I'm hurrying down the stairs to join the others." Sam's breathing gathered momentum.

"I'm outside on the front veranda. I stop and rub my hands over one of the large white wooden columns. I run down the stairs and into the garden, following the escaping crowd. Lights come on in the big house. Now shots are being fired! Panic breaks out. Everyone's screaming. I'm confused. I don't understand what's happening." Sam's chest heaved, and his body tensed. Chantley's eyes opened wide. A premonition of bad things overcame her. "The men outside are pushing the gate back and forth, but it's not opening. Slaves are trapped at the gate and shot."

"Go on," said the doctor breathlessly.

"Suddenly, the gate swings open. Someone from the inside has opened it. It's dark; I can't see who. Slaves are crossing the road into the sugarcane. I stop at the gate and see a white woman with a large key in her hand! She's holding a young man's arm, pulling him out. I look at the woman's face. It's her!"

Dr. Dwyer straightened up. "Who?"

The spell broke. Sam suddenly jumped to his feet, his eyes wide open. "It's her!" He pointed to Chantley excitedly. "She was helping everyone escape!" He bounded over, kissed her, lifted her off the ground and spun her around. Chantley felt exhilaration sweep over her body. In the dark, she barely saw Sam, but his presence felt larger-than-life—his powerful arms, musky scent and vital breath on her cheek. She held him tight, never wanting to let go, their solid embrace intensifying the blend of pure joy and such happiness that it felt almost painful, experiencing an out-of-the-body moment that rolled through her body and floated her consciousness to the tiny room's ceiling.

Everything changed. Sam's experience proved their bond to be real, to be undeniable. The crystal container of dissimulation, within which she had trapped the vanities of 'he's-just-a-friend' and 'only-a-guide,' shattered and allowed the free flow of love to rush into her now-open heart. Nothing held her back. She loved Sam and finally admitted it after weeks of denial.

"Do you understand what happened?" Sam demanded, looking at the doctor. "It's so clear! Chantley helped me escape slavery. No wonder we have such a strong connection!" He grabbed Chantley's hand and headed to the door.

"We haven't finished," exclaimed Dr. Dwyer, jumping up to her feet, her clipboard hugged tightly to her chest.

"No, Dr. Dwyer. I have all the answers I came looking for."

Chapter Fifteen

Chantley returned to her hostel room that night, barely cognizant of her actions. She sat on her bed, enveloped in thought yet unable to think clearly. The cheap ratty room acquired a special dimension. Is this what seventh heaven feels like? A numb tingling all over my body?

With their love now in the open, she felt great relief. The regression proved her suspicions: that the intense feelings of their first encounter confirmed a past connection. And Sam accepted it as well. All the insecurities about their relationship disappeared. He loved her and said so. She glowed, experiencing a thrill traveling up and down her body, yet her mind resembled pudding. Several thoughts appeared randomly, disjointedly.

She had to continue the search for her mother, but her affection for Sam turned everything around. She spun several scenarios. She could pursue a long-distance relationship with Sam or return to Sam after discovering her mother. Better yet, she could convince her mother to join them in Boulder. She smiled happily at the thought. Not only would she meet her mother, but also find a life partner. These imaginations entered and exited her mind as she sat exulting in the unexpected and shocking revelations of the day.

The following day, a message from her cell phone woke her. It came from Sam. Can I see you at 10.30 at the Starbucks on Pine near the University? She nodded her head. Of course, she replied.

Chapter Sixteen

Sam tapped his fingers impatiently on the table and stared out of the window. He kept picking up his coffee cup, raising it to his lips, and putting it down. Chantley remained patient, waiting for him to speak, and, when nothing came, intervened.

"What's going on?" she asked.

"I don't know where I'm going."

"What do you mean?"

"There are so many questions in my mind," he replied disjointedly. "I planned to stay with my family and keep looking for a job. Now everything's up in the air."

Sam's face sagged, and his eyelids hung heavy and bloated. He lifted his coffee cup and tapped his fingers some more. "I've been up all night thinking about this. What happened yesterday changed everything." He returned the untasted coffee to the saucer and looked out the window. "I've got two choices. I either forget about the whole thing, like it's some strange and inexplicable event, or accept what I saw as real. Either way, everything has changed."

She nodded her head, though bewildered. His aloofness, his way of not looking at her when speaking, and the coldness in his voice baffled her. Her stomach knotted.

"What do you mean?"

He finally looked at her. "See, here's the deal. One thing is, everything could be just something that's crazy, that's not factual." He pushed his glasses up his nose. "And the other thing is if what happened is the truth, there's no way I can let it slide; just let it go. I will need to see if it's real." He hesitated. "I mean, I like you, I like you a lot, but continuing our relationship at this point would be like ignoring the eight-hundred-pound gorilla in the room. There's no way I could make it work."

She cringed. What about the feelings between them? Yesterday, they had connected deeply and discovered something from the past that tightly bound them. It must have been deeply unsettling to go back to a place and a condition that was the source of his people's sufferings. Chantley's fingers tightened. Where did she fit in his plans?

"So, what happened yesterday didn't make any difference?" she asked, her face pale. "You're not convinced that we have a past relationship?"

He sighed deeply. "The experience was so intense and overwhelming that when I got out of bed this morning, I felt burned out. All I can find is confusion."

Chantley took her turn to look out the window. The downtown Starbucks started filling with customers coming in for their mid-morning coffee. The swish of the front doors opening and closing, the chatter of the customers waiting in line and the clatter of dishes being handled in the kitchen filled the air, but she hardly heard any of that. Rather, their small table in the corner cocooned them in a soft silence, deflecting the oncoming noise, splintering it into a million tiny pieces that floated away like specks of dust.

Clearly, Sam stood on the edge of discovery, on the border between two worlds. Naturally, he hesitated. But she never expected to be baggage on this ride. Especially after the heartfelt embrace and ardent kisses of the day before. Was this just about him? Didn't he see that the narrative included her?

The uncertainty and unease of her life before Sam's entry returned with full force. She shivered. Had she made a mistake in requesting the regression? Yesterday, she had approached it as a point to be tidied up, a tick to be marked off her to-do list before leaving town. *How foolish of me not to see where this would lead. Why did I allow myself to fall in love again? Didn't I do this before, trusting too easily?*

Her heart filled with pain. She pictured her father's grave under the trees on a ridge on the hill on which the ashram sat. Did he feel this way when he arrived there, long-haired and destitute, so many years ago? Her father had searched for shelter, as she did now, but he had not been alone. He had Mom, but more, their Guru was there. No worries, no cares, persisted in Guru-ji's presence, and all problems became very small. Guru-ji's face came into view, sitting next to her father, looking frail and old, his skin dark from the South Indian sun, smiling through his white beard. She remembered her father's words: that Guru-ji is always present and that his benign blessings remain for the taking, whether in this world or from the other. One should have faith. She breathed deeply and regained confidence.

"You can do what you want," she whispered.

"I'm sorry, I've got to go," said Sam. He pushed his chair away and, without looking back, left, abandoning his untouched coffee on the table.

The cocoon broke, and the sounds inside the café gathered into a vast wave of loud discordance that fell and crashed upon her without sympathy. Chantley held her hands against her ears as tears threatened to storm her eyes.

"Sorry, sorry," she mumbled, stumbling out of the coffee shop, brushing against customers along the way who stared at her with surprise.

Chapter Seventeen

Chantley finished packing her clothes in the small, brown, twenty-year-old Samsonite case which came with her from India. Her time in the hostel was over, and she had to leave. She counted her dollars. She had enough for the bus ticket, with a bit left over. She placed her wallet and the tin box containing her mother's photo and her relatives' addresses into her shoulder bag, slung it over her right shoulder, picked up the suitcase and headed out the door. As soon as she reached the sidewalk, her cell phone rang.

It was Sam. He sounded breathless. "I need to see you right away."

Chantley hesitated.

"Look, this is important," he insisted, "I need to see you."

She thought everything had ended. "What's it about?" she asked coldly.

"I've found out something," he replied excitedly, "about what happened back during those slave times. I think you will be interested."

"I don't think I have the time. I'm on my way to the bus terminal."

"Where are you going?"

"Pittsburgh."

"No. Please let's talk before you go. When I said it's important, I wasn't kidding."

Chantley looked at her battered suitcase. The clothes and toiletries it contained comprised the extent of her possessions. She glanced at the time on her phone. The bus wouldn't leave for another two hours.

"Okay. We can meet at the bus station. I have a few minutes before the bus leaves."

"Great! I'll see you there."

*****

Sam sat at a table next to the restaurant's front door in the Greyhound terminal. Housed in a small brick building downtown on Walnut Street, it featured large windows in the front, and red-painted metal chairs and heavy tables bolted to the floor. It served glorified fast food to passers-by. He fidgeted nervously with his fingers.

As soon as Chantley walked in, Sam jumped to his feet, rushed over and hugged her. She recoiled. He had feared this exact reaction.

"I'm sorry about what happened yesterday," he offered. "I was really confused."

Chantley said nothing and sat down. Sam went to the counter and came back with coffee for him and tea for her.

"What's this about?" she asked coldly.

He hemmed and hawed for a few seconds. "About yesterday. I apologize for what happened. For leaving you like that."

Chantley pursed her lips, the hurt obvious in her eyes. "What do you want to tell me?"

He rubbed his head. "It's not my nature to accept anything blindly. It was a hump I couldn't get over." The evening after the regression, he had lain in bed, unable to sleep. The rush of emotions at Dr. Dwyer's office had obscured a fundamental question: could he accept reincarnation as a fact? Until then, he treated it as an idiosyncrasy or a peculiar cultural construct. But, lying in the dark, staring at the ceiling, he understood it to be the central issue.

Chantley glanced at her watch. Sam understood he had to get to the point. "I thought I had only two choices: fully accept or reject the idea. But when I went over the regression, it struck me how real everything seemed: the mansion, the flowers, the sound of the rifles, the slaves—like I was physically present. I understood that another option existed."

She raised her eyebrows questioningly.

Sam straightened up, reached into a backpack on the floor next to him, pulled out an inch-thick stack of papers, dropped it on the table and looked at her expectantly. "I went to the library to do some research."

She crossed her arms and sat back. "Go ahead."

He raised his arms excitedly. "People think of slaves as helpless, quietly waiting for Northerners to rescue them, that they weren't masters of their destiny, accepting whatever fate threw at them. But that wasn't the case at all." He picked up the papers and shuffled them nervously. "My research shows that in the years before the civil war, slaves resisted their condition in many ways. They constantly escaped. So many that they formed entire villages deep in the swamps of Virginia and the Carolinas, living almost as they did in Africa. A whole culture, called Gullah or Geechee, connected to that period, is still found in lowland South Carolina. Secondly, the Spanish, who controlled Florida a hundred years before the Civil War, offered freedom to slaves who crossed the border. Did you know that thousands of slaves, especially from Georgia and South Carolina, escaped to Fort Augustine and joined the Spanish army to fight the British, who controlled America then?"

She shook her head.

He continued with excitement. "In the years before the Civil War, with no outside help, slaves formed armed groups and fought against slave owners. Dozens of skirmishes erupted as armed blacks raided plantations and freed slaves. Some free slaves even returned to the slave states to fight for their brothers. We don't hear about this, but slaves liberating themselves happened all over the South."

Sam saw the confusion on her face. Did she understand the importance of his discoveries? "And there's another thing: I checked the map, and there is a place called Cooper River near Charleston, South Carolina!"

Her eyes widened. "What does this mean?"

"The attack on the plantation, the escaping slaves and my folks being from South Carolina. Don't you see? The events I saw during the regression could be real!"

"But does this prove anything between us?" she said, shrugging her shoulders. Sam scratched his head. Did she mean to dampen his enthusiasm, to maintain distance? "There's no proof that either you or I were there."

"Aren't there too many coincidences for it not to be real?" he insisted. "Without a doubt, I saw you during the regression." Sam pointed to her middle and ring fingers. "They're the same ones I saw in my regression, holding the key."

She shook her head. "What can you do? Isn't that in the past?"

"I've made a decision. I'm going to drive to South Carolina and get to the bottom of everything. I haven't been able to sleep. I won't be able to get it out of my head until I figure out if what I saw is true."

"That's a good idea," she replied. "It makes sense for you to go. That's what you've always talked about."

Sam took a breath. "I realized last night that I'm floating around with no direction because I have no idea who I am. Once I get a clear understanding of my past, my future will become obvious." He leaned over. "I want you to come with me."

Chantley pursed her lips. Her expression was noncommittal. "I don't think..."

"But this concerns you as well," he said, finally acknowledging her role in the episode. "My being at the plantation and trying to escape is only one part. Last night, I realized that you are the final point in this journey."

"This is the first time you brought me into the picture," she remarked. "I felt like an appendage or a part of the background."

Sam took off his hat and put it on the table. "I'm sorry I made this about myself. Last night I remembered how everything started—when we first met at the Mall, and you told me we had a connection from a previous life."

With the apology, Chantley's defensiveness evaporated. "I was going to go east anyway," she said. Sam saw a crack in her resistance.

"You'll save money," he assured her. "And you won't have to travel across the country by yourself."

She nodded her head.

"Please come with me," he said. He glanced at her suitcase. "I got my stuff packed. I don't want to leave without you."

She finally smiled.

Chapter Eighteen

Sitting cross-legged on the passenger seat, with the wind blowing in from the open car window, cruising at eighty miles per hour down Interstate 25, Chantley felt relieved to have left the smog that sat like an inverted brown bowl over the great city of Denver. The sun baked the asphalt and the heat hummed along the length of the highway, but the smooth jazz on the radio and the breeze flying through her hair made her spirits soar. Travel brought excitement and anticipation. She had felt stuck, bogged down, in Boulder.

"Why are we turning here?" asked Chantley. Walsenburg, Colorado, a small nondescript town, featured the usual gas stations, fast food joints and a few stoplights. The town smelled like burnt bitumen: the summer heat singed its streets.

"We're catching highway one-sixty going west," replied Sam, "and then south on two-eighty-five at Alamosa."

"What's our destination?"

"Taos. I know some people there. We'll spend the night with them."

Sam shut the windows and turned on the air conditioning. The cold air tickled her toes and blew on her bare legs. Chantley giggled. She finally gained the courage to try a skimpy skirt that barely touched her knees. She felt like a child again, when short clothes were acceptable, before the onset of adulthood demanded modesty. In India, at least.

"Let me ask you something about reincarnation," he said.

"Go ahead." Chantley absent-mindedly kneaded a callus on her big toe, a product of the days of wandering around Boulder.

"If someone's been bad, really bad, does he come back as a cockroach?"

Chantley laughed, doubling over, her teeth flashing in the sun. "I never heard that before!" she exclaimed.

"Okay. Let me ask you a more serious question." He raised his finger. "If every soul reincarnates, how can you explain the growth in population? Fifty years ago, we had four billion people, and now it's over seven billion. How can so many new souls appear that suddenly?"

"An incredible number of souls exist. Not just people but all living things have souls. You can't imagine how many billions, trillions, of souls exist on this planet. Not just this planet but millions of planets and material universes, all containing sentient beings. Then there are spiritual universes, the original homes of all souls. The number of souls in spiritual universes is many times greater than the material ones." She kept rubbing the callus, trying to move the heaviness and bland, dull ache out of it. The skin around it showed red and thin, and the grinding made it ache.

"Wow! You got me there." He winked at her. "How about another question?"

Chantley nodded her head. She liked Sam's zeal, his openness to new things.

"When a person dies, how does the soul go to a different body? Is it like a lottery, like if you get a winning ticket, you go to a better place, but if you get a losing ticket, you end up as an animal?"

Chantley burst out laughing.

"What? This is a serious question."

She sobered up. "You're asking an important question about the connection between karma and reincarnation."

Sam brightened up. "That's right," he declared. "That's exactly what I meant."

"Of c-o-o-o-urse you did," she replied, drawing out the syllable in mild, humorous sarcasm. "Here's what happens: all our actions leave invisible imprints in our minds. Over the course of a lifetime, these imprints create patterns. Then, upon death, when the soul departs the body, these patterns and desires determine where we end up. My Guru would tell me that these desires, like airs, carry the soul to the type of body that will enable it to fulfill its destiny."

"I still don't get it."

Chantley enjoyed this conversation. It reflected the topics discussed back at the ashram. They were a philosophical bunch there, starting with her father. She had gone into town to receive a formal degree from a poor Indian imitation of the English institutions left after colonization which taught Yates and Elizabethan monarchies but little true Indian history and practically no indigenous literature to the denatured natives. Instead, her real education came from the daily afternoon talks with her father. He introduced her not only to classical Indian literature but also to how to probe life's deeper questions. "Our future bodies are dependent on what we do in this life," she replied, sighing at the thought of her father. "We get what we desire."

"So, we have to be careful about what we want?"

"Exactly."

Sam nodded his head thoughtfully. "That's a nice theory, but can you prove it? Reincarnation is just a belief, right?"

"Think of a building with a frieze or a pattern along its top."

"Like the Federal building in Denver?"

"Yes. Suppose you're standing in front of that building. Isn't it logical to expect the pattern to continue on the building's sides, even if you can't see it?"

"I see what you mean."

"We have our individual karmas, but we're also connected. We are like ships, carrying our loads, crossing each other's paths in the wide ocean."

"What about a truly evil person, such as Hitler? Isn't he in a different category altogether?"

"Yes. The texts mention various hellish and heavenly planets. Even in this world, hellish situations, places of terrible consequences, exist for people who engage in evil choices. Evil people do undergo consequences much darker and more prolonged than others. But even their karma has a point—they must learn and realize what they have done. Otherwise, what justice is there for their victims?"

"Okay, I got another question." He glanced over and smiled, creases forming around his eyes.

"This has to be good," she warned.

"This is a tough one. What's the point of karma?"

"Karma is the vehicle by which morality connects with reincarnation. We do things that hurt or benefit others, not just physically but also people's psyches, feelings, and relationships. Karma allows us to work out our issues, even if it takes many lifetimes." The explanations came naturally. She didn't have to think about them.

Sam pondered her answer. He rubbed his forehead.

"What about God's judgment? Doesn't heaven and hell also serve as an impetus for moral behavior?"

She nodded her head. "I suppose the fear or anticipation of hell or heaven would do that."

"In either case, morality is served?"

"We learn by our experiences and from our spiritual teachers. In karma, we can work out issues rather than be cast into heaven or hell eternally based on actions of just one life. It is a more reasonable theory of morality."

"What do you mean by 'work out issues'? Isn't karma completely deterministic? Fatalistic in that the chain of actions and reactions is inescapable?"

"No. At the moment of a moral dilemma or choice, we have the freedom to choose our response. After we select our alternative, then, of course, the reaction is inevitable. But at that moment of choosing, two things happen: one is the moral consequence and secondly, a moment of learning. By choosing and learning, we have freedom; freedom to grow."

Sam raised his finger again. "How about the theology of a Judgement Day? A time when people rise out of the grave and ascend to heaven or go to hell?"

"I don't know the theology," admitted Chantley. "But the idea that people suffer in their graves and then are cast into hell forever seems unfair. It doesn't allow for degrees of outcomes. Some good deeds are better than others, while some bad ones are worse. Having a limited number of moral consequences seems simplistic compared to the almost unlimited and personalized quality of karmic outcomes."

When Sam nodded his head, she recognized his coming across to her point of view. "Your explanations seem to be a more mature way of understanding morality," he said.

"In what way?"

"Judging, rewarding, punishing. Who gets judged, punished or rewarded?"

"Kids?"

"Exactly. The idea of a judging God feels a bit paternalistic. Most of us, I imagine, are adult enough to sort out issues on our own. Mature people take responsibility for their actions and work towards solving them. And I like what you say about learning. It's something obvious; it happens all the time and doesn't ask us to believe something outside our experience."

"So, you accept reincarnation?"

Sam laughed. "No. I'm not convinced yet."

They stopped at Alamosa to fill up. In less than ten minutes, they reached its outskirts. They entered a two-lane highway, driving south through the San Luis Valley, a fertile land with alfalfa and barley growing on both sides of the road, with the beautiful Sangre de Cristo mountain range miles to the left. The valley was pure country, with streams and lakes fed by the melting snow and the rain on the mountains, the temperature cooling off, and the healthy air clear of the slightest bit of urban damage. A few patches of ivory snow still clung to the tops of the blue-black peaks, which appeared one after another, mile after mile, several of them fourteeners, their sides covered with trees and thick bushes. Chantley admired the scenery for a long time and then went back to attending to the stubborn callus. She pulled, pinched and pushed it, but her efforts didn't help. The pain flared, and her toe throbbed. She took a deep breath and, resisting the urge to continue, grimaced and eased her feet back into their shoes.

"There are a lot of bears here," Sam remarked.

"Where?" she asked, straightening up and scanning the sides of the road as if expecting one to pop up immediately. "Have you seen any?"

Sam suppressed his laughter. "Yes," he replied, "a couple of times. Once we leave this valley, we'll enter a national forest. Not just bears, but mountain lions." He pointed his finger at a building down a dirt road to the right as they whizzed past. "See that?"

She swung her head around. The small church, built of whitewashed adobe, featuring a large brass bell hanging from a wooden beam set in a circular opening in the wall above the front door, sat in a pretty courtyard filled with flowers.

"It's an old Spanish mission, several hundred years old. All this area used to belong to Mexico. A lot of the people here are originally Spanish. Many Indians also live here, especially in the hills near Taos."

"Indian!" exclaimed Chantley, "Indians?"

Sam guffawed. "Not your kind of Indians."

"Then who?"

"Native Americans."

"Really?"

"Yes. Many of these areas are sacred to them. Further west, in the mountains, are hot springs with high mineral content. The Native Americans consider them to be sacred. They would drink the spring waters. They claim it cures diseases."

"That makes sense."

"This area attracts many spiritual people," continued Sam.

"Yes!" she responded, brightening up. "I can feel it. This place has a real spiritual quality."

*****

Two hours after leaving Walsenburg, they arrived in Antonito, a small town at the south end of the San Luis Valley. A few miles north of the New Mexico border, it nestled in a small valley low enough for several streams to flow through, yet high enough for fresh air from the Sangre de Cristo range to sweep through.

Sam spied a sandwich shop. They bought their eatables, discovered a small park with picnic tables scattered under cottonwood trees and sat facing each other. Chantley removed her runners and rubbed her feet in the grass, relishing its softness against her overheated toes. She stretched her legs, letting the muscles pull, enjoying the burn as she held them tight and, upon letting go, the deliciousness of relaxation. She purred.

"How are you feeling?" asked Sam.

Chantley peered into the trees for a second, reflecting. "Surprised at how everything turned out. Yesterday, I pictured myself in a bus, all alone, heading off to Pittsburgh, where I don't know a soul."

"And now?"

"Here we are, driving in your car all the way to South Carolina!"

"Which do you prefer?"

"Being with you, of course!" As soon as Chantley spoke, she blushed. Being candid was an American thing. It had taken a year for her to tell Vijay that she loved him. I'm becoming American, she thought, with both wonder and alarm. In India, she would never have traveled alone with a man. *I must have inherited this independent nature from my mother.*

In India, a formality existed as to how women and men connected. Everyone—parents, relatives and friends—got involved. How one fit into a matrix of family, caste and community defined one's identity, and the first question asked upon meeting someone new always concerned spouse, family and kinship. In India, she was terribly misfit: with both parents gone and, after Guru-ji's death and the community losing focus, having neither elders nor society to settle things for her. This explained why everything failed with Vijay. In a way, she understood his family's predicament. With no parents they could relate to, no caste to support her, and no greater community to which she belonged, they didn't know where to place her and, thus, how she fit in with them. It doomed her to failure even before starting.

She knew, before coming, that Americans would be different. American visitors at the ashram defined themselves by their ambitions, accomplishments, and careers. Indians thought of Americans as selfish, based on their rugged individualism, which trumped family relations, friends and society. Being inconsiderate of social demands, not to speak of abandoning parents and grandparents to old-age homes, was seen by Indians as being ungrateful and their individualism, awful.

Chantley had a theory about this. During America's colonization, young men and women left their families to settle on the frontier at an early age. It resulted in a high demand for eligible women. Because of the seller's market, women had the freedom to make choices that those in old societies didn't—attitudes, which became embedded in the American psyche over time.

While Chantley had no place in Indian social customs, it did not prevent her from being wary of American ones. Relationships in India generally worked well and lasted long. She heard of girls having boyfriends, sometimes even live-in boyfriends, in big cities like Mumbai and New Delhi, but this didn't happen in the vast majority of the country. The shame such an act would bring upon their families! In America, the level of family turmoil—divorces and intergenerational conflicts—scared her. *But, of course, this doesn't absolve Indian social traditions of their share of unfairness.*

Thus, while enjoying Sam's company and exploring her unfolding freedom, she still retained a deep-seated wariness. She wouldn't feel entirely comfortable until she understood what brought them together. Her eyelids flickered. *This is the purpose of our trip.*

"I'm glad you came. I'm really enjoying your company," said Sam. He walked over, held her hands and bent over and kissed her as she looked up at him questioningly. She smiled but looked away.

"Is everything okay?" asked Sam.

She nodded her head but still avoided eye contact.

"No, it's not." Sam hemmed and hawed for several seconds. "I don't know how to put this, but do you feel uncomfortable because of my race?"

Chantley regarded him with surprise. "It's nothing like that," she replied.

"It's not easy for me either."

She gazed at him, puzzled.

"There's a taboo about interracial relationships, especially between black men and white women. While it can be dangerous to black men, white women also face hostility."

"Why is that?"

Sam laughed. "That's why I like you. In America, there's so much B.S. about race and gender. You don't bring any of that."

Chantley looked at him blankly.

Sam returned to his seat. "Relationships are hard enough, to begin with. And more so when family members object."

"Family?"

"Many white parents would object to their daughter dating a black man."

Chantley suddenly wondered how her mother and father would react to her situation. She had never questioned their attitudes.

"The same thing with black families. The attitude one gets is: isn't your own kind good enough?"

Chantley pondered Sam's statements. "What's at the heart of this?"

"It started when whites and blacks were first thrown together. Back then, most white Americans thought of slaves as chattel. Blacks were at the bottom, and whites on top. To this day, relationships can be traced back to this narrative. When a black man dates a white woman, it upsets the so-called 'natural order' of things. It's an usurpation of rank, of power. And to restore this order, it had to be suppressed, even violently."

Sam's exposition didn't unsettle Chantley. On the contrary, she related to his sense of being an outsider.

Sam continued. "One thought has been going around in my mind for the past few days. When I saw you at the plantation gate, I stopped dead in my tracks, not because you were holding the gate open for the slaves to escape, but because of a sense of recognition. When I looked into your eyes, it stirred many feelings, not just surprise. There's something more. How could a black slave have a connection to a white woman back then? What does it mean?"

"Isn't that why you asked me to come with you?"

"One of the reasons," admitted Sam. "There's a mystery in both our lives that demands explanation." Sam took Chantley's hand. "The other reason is I'm loving being with you!"

Sam reached down and kissed her. This time, she didn't fight it. She closed her eyes and allowed the delicious sweetness of his affection to sweep through her. Did the convergence of their goals and their travels lead them to synchronicity? Did her relationship with Sam, so unexpected and filled with meaningful coincidences, indicate an intangible yet irrefutable connection?

*****

They entered Carson National Forest at the south end of San Luis valley, and the highway began its climb as the car's gears felt the strain. Large red boulders and gnarled pinyon pines, twisted and brown, with their tops sporting spiny green crowns, abounded. Red willow, spruce, and pine dotted the hills. At this elevation, the thin air glowed magically in the late afternoon sun, sparkling like golden wine. As the road crested a hill, Chantley saw below a striking blue tributary of the Rio Grande, twisting around an orange-brown rock the size of an apartment building. It circled into a tiny valley just big enough to hold the waterway, its banks lined with birch and the steep hills covered with evergreen bushes. She soaked in the magical scene.

Their approach took them to the top of a high hill that oversaw the entire area, spread out below like a gigantic bowl. Taos, surrounded by ranches and farms, situated itself on a bit of flat land at the bottom of this geological structure, while the Rio

Grande ran down and south through the valley. The sun hung low on the horizon when they reached the bottom.

Chapter Nineteen

John and Lori lived in a small house in the eastern part of Taos. A ten-foot-high fence made of thin wooden poles, held together with wire, enclosed the white-adobe house. A garden of wildflowers, now in full bloom—purple, white, yellow and blue—grew in front, and a path of brown shale guided Sam and Chantley to antique wooden front doors featuring large circular brass handles.

Lori greeted them with a smudge—a roll of lighted sage—from which wafted a purifying smoke. Chantley spread her hands over and gathered it towards her, raising her hands to her face.

"How did you know how to do that?" asked Lori.

Chantley stopped with surprise. A reflex action, a familiar sacred gesture, reminded her of the aarti lamp used in worship at the ashram.

"I grew up in India," she offered. "We have a similar thing there."

Lori ushered them into the living room. A field-stone fireplace leaned against the wall, red wooden beams ran along the ceiling, and sunny, yellow-cream tile lined the floor. Plenty of rugs lay all around. Three light brown sofas, stationed perpendicularly to each other in a U-shaped formation, faced the fireplace. Photographs of their children, hoops of wild grass, woven artwork and brightly painted Southwestern clay objects hung on the walls. They sat down to steaming mugs of chamomile tea.

"Thank you for coming," said John. Long and lean, with a bald head and closely-cropped thin gray beard, he wore a red checkered flannel shirt while Lori, slightly plump, with gray-streaked hair, strong dark eyes, tanned skin and a well-creased face, stood a couple of inches shorter than her husband. They made a sweet couple.

"I'm glad I finally came here," said Sam. "I met John in Boulder three years ago while he attended a summer intensive creative writing course at Naropa University," he explained to Chantley.

John introduced himself. "I got my degree from Boston University forty years ago. After that, I couldn't settle down. I had to get away from it all, and like generations before, it was 'Go west, young man.' Back in the '60s, Taos was quite the hippie hangout, a sort of Haight-Ashbury in the hills." He rubbed his smooth head and laughed. "Back then, my hair hung down to my elbows."

Chantley smiled. His words brought back her earliest recollections of her father and his long hair. She hadn't connected him to the hippie movement. Maybe he wasn't as eccentric as she had imagined.

"When I arrived here, I didn't need to travel anymore. I knew I had found my home."

"Why don't we visit the Pueblo tomorrow morning?" asked Sam.

Chantley looked around questioningly. Pueblo?

Lori lifted a painting from the wall and showed it to her. The Pueblo on the canvas resembled an apartment building of sorts, with cube-shaped blocks made of brown clay, built on top of each other. The sun threw long shadows on a large square, and on its far end ran a creek, over which rested a bridge.

"My family owns a home there," she said, revealing her Native American heritage. "It's the longest inhabited building in America, and the Tiwa, as we call ourselves, have lived there for over a thousand years."

The idea of living in such an ancient place fascinated Chantley. "How did you like living there?" she asked.

"As a child, I loved it. It's a real community, and we've kept our traditions—festivals and sacred days. We lived there mostly during the summers. But there's no electricity or even piped water. The community wants to keep it that way. That's why my parents had another house outside. But when I married John, I decided to move into town. We have a son and daughter; he's moved to Los Angeles, and our girl lives in Santa Fe."

"How did you meet Chantley?" asked John. Sam explained. They listened, fascinated, glancing at Chantley occasionally, nodding their heads.

"That's quite a story," exclaimed Lori. "I understand what you say about past lives. We feel our ancestors live with us in an invisible form: we seek their guidance in our lives. Without their spirits and those of the animals, our existence would be lonely."

Lori glanced at her watch. "Why don't we have dinner?" she asked. She led them to a large dining room, occupied by a table of thick cottonwood stained a golden brown, surrounded by eight wooden chairs with full backs and strong legs. Lori brought steaming homemade tortillas from the oven, filling the room with the scent of warm bread. On the table sat the fillings: small shiny-red ripe tomatoes sliced into quarters, roasted red and green peppers, black pinto beans soaked overnight, soft brown beans, sharp homemade queso, cooked rice garnished with green coriander and seasoned with lime butter, guacamole, carnitas, a boat of sour cream and chopped jalapenos.

Chantley observed the others. The bread resembled a chapatti, but instead of scooping the condiments with its small torn pieces, they piled the ingredients in the middle of the tortilla before wrapping the whole thing up. She passed on the carnitas, heaped the vegetables, beans, rice and queso, folded her burrito, and poured a smoky salsa verde prepared with charred green tomatillos and roasted sweet corn, on top.

The discussion over dinner returned to the Pueblo and the people's customs. "Among the Tiwa, we follow both our traditional religion and Roman Catholicism," Lori said. "When the Spanish came here in the mid-1500s, they built a church in the pueblo, without permission, using conscripted Indian labor. The missionaries were dismissive and disrespectful of our traditions. Public beheadings and torture of spiritual leaders led to several revolts. After the Spanish-American war, New Mexico became part of America, but the Pueblo's struggle continued."

"Why?" questioned Chantley.

"Because of the deep suspicion indigenous beliefs raised in America," answered John. "Did you know that in 1883, the federal government passed a law called 'The Religious Crimes Act'? It made the practice of Native American religions illegal. In fact, up until 1935, Native Americans could be fined or imprisoned for practicing their traditional beliefs."

"That's shocking!" exclaimed Sam.

"Couldn't anything be done?" questioned Chantley.

"No," replied Lori. "We weren't granted citizenship until 1924, and thus, not allowed to vote. Who would defend us in the political system? The law created hostility to Native religions and cultures in all branches of the government, not to speak of ordinary Americans. It didn't stop there. Residential schools, mostly run by missionary organizations and financially supported by the government, replaced the original cultures and religions with Western ones."

Chantley remembered her Indian history of Hindu temples destroyed, Brahmins killed or driven away, with years of suppression and forced conversions during the Portuguese Inquisition in Goa.

The six hundred years of subjugation of India by various Islamic empires, followed by colonial rule for another two hundred years, remain visible to this day. The statues of Buddha demolished, great universities such as Nalanda burned down, and its' monks beheaded, resulted in a fragmented culture, people reduced to penury and the country's original beliefs under constant siege. But that was the point of it all. "In a way, it's inevitable that these things happened," she stated.

"What do you mean?" asked John.

"Inherent in colonization is the belief that the conquered have to reject their original attachments. As long as the subjected are spiritually attached to their land, they would never be fully colonized." She glanced at Lori. "It's always about the land, isn't it?"

"Absolutely," agreed Lori. "All Native American religions have deep connections to the earth. For us, the spiritual and material overlap; they inhabit the same space. Thousands of sacred places dot this continent."

"I can relate to that," said Chantley. "When I was thirteen, I went on a pilgrimage through parts of South and North India with my friends."

"People still do that?"

"Yes. Pilgrimages are popular in India because the land still holds sacred connotation." She remembered her travels. They took her to temples on top of hills, deep forests and the sides of cliffs. In Tirupati, she climbed two thousand three hundred steps, a distance of four miles, to the top of Tirumala hill to see the Deity there. In Haridwar, she took an early morning bath in the holy Ganges. In Rajasthan, she performed aarti, the worship of Dev Narayan, the Deity of the sacred forests of that region.

"That must have been exciting! What did you do on the pilgrimage?" asked John.

"Each place had a temple dedicated to the Deity of that land. Pundits there related stories of the Deities and the lives of holy men who had meditated there. We learned the connections each spot had with the heroes from the Mahabharata or the Ramayana, the ancient epics of India." She glanced at Lori. "I think the civilizational idea of India exists in this sacred geography rather than in history textbooks or exhortations to patriotism."

"I understand what you're saying," said Lori. "You know, I've seen pictures of Hindu Deities. So many of them. We, too, have many Deities in our religion."

Chantley smiled. "Western missionaries complain that Hinduism contains three hundred million Deities. The actual count is probably larger given the unfathomable number of sacred sites and their associated histories." They all laughed.

"How exactly do you relate to Deities?" asked Sam.

Chantley wondered how to reply in a way that all could understand. "My Guru-ji depicted a radically different view of reality. Instead of a bleak world devoid of meaning, he presented a world full of personalities, some human, some fully divine and others, representatives of natural forces. For example, the Ganges is not just a body of water but is also a female spiritual divinity, named Ganga Ma, who dresses in a white sari with a crimson lotus in one hand and a water pot in the other. The Sun possesses similar features—besides giving light, heat, and energy, it is likewise a personality named Surya Dev." She remembered his teachings. The world's features, whether rivers, mountains, or seas, are represented by Deities, each with their particular narrative, through which humans could form a personal bond with the sacred place.

"Connecting to the land through Deities is very much in line with our beliefs," agreed Lori.

Chantley wasn't surprised. Why shouldn't a similar understanding exist in traditional cultures throughout the world?

"But isn't there a single, unitary principle?" asked Sam.

"All Deities are seen as representatives of a Supreme God," Chantley explained. "Both unity and diversity exist, not just one or the other."

"You have a remarkable understanding of Indian culture," remarked John. "Thank you!"

Chantley beamed. She felt her shyness disappear and her confidence blossom. The gathering took a more intimate turn, where her words and opinions were welcomed and not judged as foreign or strange. "What connection do modern Americans have with the land?" she asked.

"Most Americans are very patriotic and have a deep personal connection to the country," replied John. "But I'd say that early on, especially during British colonial times, the emotional connection remained with Britain. Settlers looked at America as an alien land to be remade in the image of the old country. That's why you have names like New England and New York. Much of this remaking was looked upon in religious terms—that the land had to be conquered and natives converted to attain God's benediction. The light of God shone on the land controlled by the colonists, while that under the Native American control remained under darkness. People thought they were doing God's work. It seems like a strange idea, but, back then, it was very real and gave power to westward expansion."

"Is the Pueblo a sacred place for the Tiwa?" Chantley asked.

"Our most revered place, Blue Lake or 'Ma-Wha-Lo' in Tiwa, is not far from here," Lori replied. "From its waters, all souls emerge and return."

The idea of life emerging from primordial waters was familiar to Chantley. Traditional cultures around the world share similar archetypes.

Lori continued. "Back in 1906, President Teddy Roosevelt took Blue Lake and about fifty thousand acres of land from the tribe. Logging companies wanted the timber around it. American capitalism, which profited from the acquisition of natural resources of the entire continent at little or no cost, became our other great opponent. The government offered compensation for the land, but the Tiwa refused it. It wasn't about money. It was about regaining our spiritual roots. Finally, in 1970, Congress returned Blue Lake to the Tiwa."

"That's great!" exclaimed Chantley.

"The important thing is that the Pueblo fought the government on the basis of the sacredness of Blue Lake," explained John. "Back in the day, it had to be a crazy strategy, but the Pueblo leadership insisted on it because it rightly described the relationship to the land. It set a precedent for self-determination for all American Indian tribes and aboriginal struggles worldwide." Chantley gauged Lori's reaction. More than joy, her face showed a sense of satisfaction and validation.

"Wow!" remarked Sam. "This is a remarkable success for a tribe in America, isn't it? It's nice to have good news, especially after everything that happened."

Chantley's eyes glazed over. The heat of the day and the journey's distance caught up with her. She unsuccessfully tried to stifle a yawn. "Sorry," she said sheepishly.

"You must be tired!' said Lori. "Let me show you to your beds."

*****

The following day resembled any other in the Southwest: all azure skies and saffron sun. After a quick breakfast, they climbed into John's 1979 Impala, which boasted a recent baby-blue paint job, new wire rims and fresh wax while retaining the original engine and interior. The backseat measured long enough to lie on, but the fabric along its edges felt worn. It handled like a boat on choppy waters, but that just made the ride memorable. The Pueblo lay not more than fifteen minutes away.

"A bunch of communes hung around town," related John. "Let's see. 'New Buffalo' was featured in the movie Easy Rider and another, 'The Hog Farm,' was started by Wavy Gravy."

"What the hell is Wavy Gravy?" asked Sam.

"He's an original hippie. He was into LSD and pranking the Establishment!"

They drove into the Pueblo grounds, parked the car, paid the entrance fee and entered the village, where a guide greeted them. A local, he waved to Lori, and she nodded back. He dressed in what could be called Aboriginal chic: black hair reaching his chest, a feathered Panama on his head, a heavy Native American silver chain with lapis lazuli around his neck, a khaki-colored shirt, a brown leather belt with a large metal buckle featuring a coyote howling at the moon, blue jeans and orange-neon Nikes. He proved pleasant and professional—he obviously did this for a living.

They walked to the middle of the large square, and Sam took in the scene. A reddish-brown building dominated the north side. Five stories high, the dwellings on the ground floor had doors, and some had windows, but the two topmost floors had none. According to the guide, originally, none had openings—individual units were entered through openings on the roof, accessible by ladders that could be pulled up in case of emergencies, such as an attack by other tribes or the Spanish. No passages existed through the walls—each home remained self-contained. On the other side of the Rio de Taos, a creek to the south side of the square stood a smaller, similar building. In the warm sun and clear air, the place shone with an inexplicable timelessness. Sam breathed deeply, inhaling its essence.

The guide walked them through one of the several open doors in the Pueblo. A small shop selling dream-catchers, silver, smooth stone jewelry and an assortment of mythical, bent-over, flute-playing figures known as Kokopellis, prevalent in the Southwest, occupied the front room. A curtain of hanging beads hid the living quarters.

"Do you want anything?" asked an old white-haired lady. She offered Chantley a still-warm circular loaf of homemade bread, cooked in a horno, a round wood-fired clay oven, sitting out in front, while Sam bought a dream catcher for his car.

The guide took them to the adobe-constructed Mission of San Geronimo near the west wall. Inside the old-fashioned Spanish Catholic church were statues of Jesus, Mary, and San Geronimo, or Saint Jerome, as he was known in English. Sam asked the priest about the Pueblo's religious convictions. He claimed no contradiction existed between Catholicism and the Tiwa's original beliefs. The tourists, satisfied, moved on.

"That's it," said Lori as they exited. "We've covered the Pueblo." The guide shook their hands and waved goodbye.

Sam checked his cell phone. It has taken an hour and a half. Still, questions crowded his mind. "What's the future for the community?" he asked.

"In many ways, we've done well," replied Lori. "But some of today's challenges are more insidious."

John clarified. "Now we have globalization—the secular, materialist descendent of colonization. MacDonald's restaurants in Taos import beef from Amazonian plantations, Starbucks' introduce coffee beans from Kenya and KFC which ships chickens from South Carolina. This destroys the intimate connection that the tribe had with the land and changes economic and social structures."

Sam recognized John's description. Instead of nations militarily taking over others while mixing in concepts of racial and religious supremacy, the impulse had become purely economic, driven by multinational corporations.

"The intimate, sustainable connection with our land is becoming superfluous."

"How is that?" Sam asked.

"Supporting a globalized lifestyle means participating in the wage-based economy. After all, grocery stores want to get paid in cash, and as northern New Mexico isn't exactly a hotspot for employment, many people are poor. So the wage-based economy creates a few winners and many losers."

Lori nodded her head in agreement. "Our economy was based on a community effort, whether in farming or hunting. Now, elders and traditional wisdom are losing value. We used to share everything. At present, it has shifted to daily work, and this affects our culture and family relationships."

"That's why your children moved away?" asked Chantley.

Sam marveled at her intuition.

Lori nodded her head. "I wish they stayed. I understand they had to find jobs, but I worry. I tried to pass our language and culture on to them. Unlike most tribes, we have schools that teach the Tiwa language and culture, but it's still difficult. The kids spent time watching TV shows, on social media or playing video games, none of which is part of our culture." She shook her head sadly. "How many parents have won the battle against 'Call of Duty' or 'Assassin's Creed'?"

Chapter Twenty

They drove south on Highway 285 for seven and a half hours, past Santa Fe, through the dark desert sands at Albuquerque, across sunbaked southern New Mexico and into the Texas panhandle at El Paso, where they caught Interstate 10 going east.

The blistering Chihuahuan desert featured some of the most empty and desolate land Chantley had ever seen. It seemed unimaginable for so much country to exist without a sign of human habitation. In India, even in the wild, it was impossible to drive more than an hour without coming across signs of human activity.

"We have to stop," she finally exclaimed, feeling as hot and desiccated as a potato chip abandoned on the car seat, her tongue gritty, with dehydration cracking her lips.

"I saw a sign for a lake a couple of miles back," said Sam, slowing down. He turned around and, minutes later, exited the paved highway and onto a dirt road which, after a seven-mile drive, ended on the banks of a small cerulean-blue lake. Set among golden-brown hills, its surface remained calm enough to perfectly mirror the small cotton-ball clouds moving low in the sky, colored purple by the setting sun.

When the car rolled to a stop, trailing dust, Chantley ran to the water's edge, took off her shoes and stepped in, the cool waves lapping deliciously at her toes. The temperature finally felt bearable with dusk's arrival, and the breeze blowing off the lake sent a tremor of delight down her body.

Sam joined her and entwined his fingers with hers. Chantley's heart thrilled at the unexpected romantic gesture. His hands clasped the small of her back. He drew her closer. She laughed and pulled away.

"Let's swim," she said. She returned to the car, changed into a one-piece black swimsuit, and stepped out.

Sam whistled as she instinctively covered her chest with her hands. "You're one hot mama," he declared.

Her cheeks turning red, she ran into the water and gasped as coolness enveloped her. She swam about a hundred yards, to the middle of the lake, with Sam following. He came beside her, and they floated on their backs, gazing into the quickly-darkening sky. Sam held out his right arm, and she rested her head on it, using her left arm to clasp his shoulder. His powerful biceps and muscular torso revealed a strength so far concealed by his intellect. She ran her fingers along his neck and shoulders, tracing the curvature of his body as hers washed up against his. For the first time since her arrival in America, she felt no stress or anxiety about her future. Becoming totally at ease with Sam, she crossed the bridge between initial awkwardness to acceptance, from searching for hints and clues to feeling mentally relaxed.

Is he the one? Would I spend the rest of her life with him? Of course, they had known each other for just one month, but he made her feel wanted and comfortable in a way that Vijay never did. She rejected the thought. Vijay is history. With Sam, she felt completely protected.

Slowly treading the water, she looked up at the sky, the stars now visible. Scattered in the inky-purple cosmos, they looked lonely—in India, stars crowded the heavens. But if the stars felt lonesome, she did not. She closed her eyes, hearing the water's soft splashing, feeling invigorated as great contentment washed over her. She reveled in the quiet of the darkness, the grounding of her spirit, after the day-long rumble of the car and the rattle of the highway. She found Sam's body brushing up against hers so comforting. He rubbed his toes against hers in the dark. She sighed.

Suddenly, a fish jumped, splashing unexpectedly, just a few feet away. Her reverie rudely interrupted, Chantley clung to Sam.

"You're awake! I thought you'd fallen asleep," he said.

"If I could, I'd stay here all night," she proclaimed. But the spell had broken. "Let's go back to the shore."

They returned, and Sam built a fire on the sand using some hard dry driftwood cluttering the beach. Chantley pulled the loaf of bread bought at the Pueblo, a brick of cheese, and two cans of tomato soup from the car's trunk. Never did grilled cheese sandwiches and soup taste so good! She felt ravenous, having had nothing to eat since breakfast in Taos, except for a bag of chips bought at a roadside gas station near Las Cruces in New Mexico. Between them, the loaf quickly disappeared.

Satisfied, she lay on her back on the sand and breathed deeply. A fresh wind blew off the lake, and chilled by the swim, she shivered.

"I'll get a blanket from the car," volunteered Sam.

"That's okay," replied Chantley. "We should head off and find a motel for the night."

"No, we'll spend the night here. I've got my tent. I can set it up."

Chantley caught her breath. With darkness setting, the lake and its surroundings, though beautiful, felt wild and untamed. Not a single evidence of humanity presented itself. Suddenly, the waters looked black and the shores, away from the flickering fire, threatening. "What about bears and mountain lions," she questioned, her anxiety rising.

Sam laughed. "Don't worry. I've done a lot of camping. We'll be fine if we don't keep food in the tent." He walked over to the car, opened the trunk and tossed her the keys as he pulled out the tent and deposited it on the beach.

She had been just ten. A young man from the village had wandered into the jungle one day, and the next morning, the villagers returned with the body. She had pushed her way through a circle of wailing relatives. The leopard's violence on the dead body had shocked her. She had spent the entire day crying. "I'd feel more comfortable in a hotel or motel," she said.

"It's too late to get back on the highway and start looking for a place to stay. Besides, we'll save at least eighty or ninety dollars."

"I'll pay for it," she offered. She had never slept in the wild. It was something just not done.

"It makes no sense," answered Sam. "We're in the middle of nowhere." He glanced at his cell phone. "Besides, I can't check the internet here. There's no way of knowing where the next motel is. We'd drive around for maybe two or three hours before finding anything."

His stubbornness surprised Chantley. Is it because I'm offering to pay? Sam has always been in charge. Does he resent my taking control? Tears flowed from her eyes. Vijay never treated me like this.

Sam reacted with alarm. "Are you okay?"

"I've never spent a night sleeping in the country. Why are you being so stubborn?"

"I didn't realize that you're so scared." The words sounded impatient.

"It's like you only see things from your point of view," she complained.

"Okay, let's get in the car," he snapped.

"You're acting as if I'm forcing you."

"No. Let's go search for your motel." He picked the tent from the beach and shoved it into the trunk.

*****

For a half-hour, not speaking a single word, Sam drove along the pitch-black highway without coming across another vehicle. Did he misinterpret the situation? He did try to reason with her. On the other hand, maybe he was at fault. He had fallen deeply in love for the first time and didn't know how to approach her. His lack of romantic experience hurt.

"You're angry, aren't you?" she finally asked.

"Just frustrated. I get that you've had a sheltered life, and you're new to this country, but you have to adapt." Sam rubbed his head. "Anyway, it got a bit out of hand."

Chantley glumly nodded her head.

"I was only trying to save some money," explained Sam.

"But I offered to pay for it."

Sam kept quiet. Maybe he had been too insistent, but the few hundred dollars in her purse wouldn't last a week or two. She didn't know what she was up against. He had packed the tent for just such occasions, for her sake.

"You act like you're always in charge, making all the decisions," she complained.

Sam felt baffled. "But I agreed to look for a motel," he pointed out.

"The way I see it," she continued, "you don't take my feelings into account."

"It's not like that. I didn't mean to hurt your feelings." He scratched his head. Sometimes she felt warm and inviting, and sometimes she retreated. *What's going on with her*, he wondered.

Chantley sighed. "I was raised in a community, surrounded by people who cared about me," she explained. "It's not my culture to be out in the jungle at night."

Of course! *I didn't take into account her cultural background.* Sam stroked his chin. It would take more time for both of them. "We don't have the sense of community you have in India. Here, everyone fends for themselves." He glanced at her. "Don't take things so seriously. I'll learn to deal with the cultural differences."

He felt stupid. It had been a silly argument. About nothing, really. Did Chantley's sensitivity reflect her troubles of the past couple of years? Did that explain her fragility? She looked at him and lightened up. He saw the change in her eyes.

"If you want a meaningful relationship, you need to treat me as an equal," she said.

Sam felt non-plussed. *When didn't I treat her as an equal?* He decided not to contradict her. "I'll do better," he promised. "I apologize."

"I welcome your apology," she said. "Thank you."

Sam smiled with relief upon her calm delivery. Two and a half hours later, just after midnight, they came across accommodations for the night.

Chapter Twenty-one

By the time they rolled into Houston, the time of day and the weather changed: the clock read four-thirty and the temperature ninety-five degrees. The South Texas landscape exchanged flat land, lakes and trees for the panhandle's hills, desert and sand. Chantley opened the car window, her lungs exulting in the moisture.

"This place reminds me of Mumbai," she exclaimed, finding the heat and humidity bracing. "I like it!"

Sam wiped his brow. "I'm glad you do, but I'm a Colorado boy. I'd never be able to stand living here."

Incredibly spread out, Houston seemed to go on forever, with sprawling highways and acres upon acres of paved roads. Clumps of buildings appeared unexpectedly, and after several miles, another bundle of structures materialized. They turned south on Interstate 45 towards downtown, exited on Dowling Street in the Greater Third Ward, and entered a wide-open, suburban neighborhood full of old houses, small shops, and overgrown recreational areas. Upon coming across a park filled with people, music and cooking aromas, they rolled to a stop.

"Let's take a look," suggested Chantley.

Revelers, mostly well-dressed black families and their children, all in a joyous spirit, packed the place. The recreational area featured a baseball diamond where many families gathered around their barbecues while a jazz ensemble performed at a bandstand. They strolled to the other side of the park and entered a lawn filled with rows of white plastic chairs occupied by dignified-looking church folk, the ladies in dresses and the men in suits, facing a cream-colored tent draped over a stage.

"What's going on?" asked Chantley. "It looks like we arrived in the middle of a celebration."

A gray-haired lady clothed in a mauve dress and jacket, with a matching pillbox hat and glasses, looked up. "It's Juneteenth."

"What's that?"

"Our pastor, Reverend Brown, will speak about that. We're from the congregation of the Missionary Baptist Church. We'll have a picnic after the sermon."

"Thank you, ma'am," replied Sam. They sat down next to her. Reverend Brown walked onto the stage and stopped at the lectern, where he placed his Bible. He wore a black tuxedo with satin lapels, a white linen shirt, well-pressed black pants, shiny leather shoes and a thin black tie. In his late fifties, tall, strong-jawed and clean-shaven, he looked as if he had attended one church picnic too many.

He tapped the microphone. "We are gathered here today to celebrate the independence of the black man in America," he started softly.

Sam looked up with interest.

"Most folks think that the black man got liberation with the signing of the Emancipation Proclamation by President Abraham Lincoln."

"No, no," murmured the crowd.

"No," echoed the Pastor. "Lincoln's Proclamation freed slaves in the Confederate States in rebellion. But that excluded the five border states, not in active rebellion, including Texas." The pastor stared at the gathering. "Did you know that over two hundred and fifty thousand slaves lived in this state at the end of the civil war?"

The crowd nodded their heads.

"Two years after the Emancipation Proclamation, at the end of the Civil War, General Granger of the Union Army arrived with two thousand soldiers at Galveston Island, just a few miles from this spot. On this very day of June nineteenth, in the great year of eighteen hundred and sixty-five, he ordered the emancipation of all slaves in Texas and thus put an end to slavery in America once and for all."

"Hear, hear," said the congregation.

The pastor's voice, rich and smooth, pronounced every syllable in full. He impressed Sam. It brought memories of his church services with his mother during his youth. He had enjoyed those sermons before discovering other voices.

"On that day of liberation, black folks in Texas rejoiced greatly. Many left their old plantations and set off for new lives. Others returned to where they once toiled, but this time, as paid workers. Great celebrations occurred spontaneously throughout the city. Families gathered, cooked food, prayed and sang gospel. And thus was born the celebration of Juneteenth."

"But it wasn't without obstruction," continued the preacher, his voice rising and gathering momentum. "After slavery came segregation. Houston wouldn't allow us to celebrate in its parks, which they said was for whites only. But did that stop us?" he questioned rhetorically.

"No," answered the congregation.

"We came together and pooled our pennies and our dollars, and in 1872, a group led by Reverend Jack Yates bought these ten acres at the corner of Dowling and Elgin for the princely sum of eight hundred dollars and named it Emancipation Park. Every year, we hold our parade and observe our celebrations here. Now America celebrates Juneteenth—in Washington D.C, Minnesota, Detroit, California and even outside the U.S. of A."

The audience, getting warmed up, clapped loudly. Sam paid keen attention.

"But our history did not start with Emancipation Day," stated the preacher, his voice rising, his sermon finding gear. "No, it started way back before that." He leaned over and, in a hushed voice, said, "It started way back in Africa."

"Hear, hear."

"It started with great mother Africa; our mother who gave birth to all of her little black children, our great crying mother whose children were snatched from her bosom and cruelly put into slave ships.

"They took us from all parts of West Africa, Nigeria, Sierra Leone, and the Gold Coast. They captured us from the villages, homes, and kingdoms."

The preacher hit his stride. "And they put us in chains and shackles, the little children, the mothers and the young men, and loaded us into ships to make the Middle Passage to America.

"Young children snatched from their families. Young women shackled in the holds of slave ships for months, suffering sickness and disease. Food not even fit for animals. People dying in their chains in the holds. Over four million died on this dark passage." The pastor wiped his forehead. "Dozens died on each ship, and they threw the dead into the dark sea, and the bones of black bodies lie at the bottom of the cold Atlantic."

"Lord, save their souls."

The preacher stopped for dramatic effect. "But that's not all. Once the slave ships arrived in America, they sold us away. Mothers separated from children, husbands from wives, and brothers from sisters. They sent us away to Virginia, Alabama, Mississippi and Texas. They cast us away to Tennessee, the Carolinas, Louisiana and Georgia."

"Lord have mercy," said the congregation.

"This was a crime." He roared. "A crime against humanity. A sin that made the good Lord shed tears that rained down from the heavens and washed away the dirt and grime of our suffering. And you know what happened?"

"What's that?"

"Out of this crucible of suffering and from the Lord's tears was born a new black man in America!"

"Hallelujah!"

The pastor pointed his forefinger into the air, jabbing it back and forth. "You see, we worked this land. We cleared the country; we grew rice, cotton and tobacco. We harvested peanuts, wheat and sugarcane. Our sweat, our blood, made this land bountiful.

"Generations of black men. Women who worked in the fields, cooked, cleaned and raised children—not just their own but also their masters'. We moved west and became ranchers, farmers and buffalo soldiers. We shaped this land. With our hands and our labor, we created America. And you know what happened?"

"What's that?'

"America created us. Out of the graves of those Africans, out of the work of those slaves, out of the enterprise of the freemen, a new black man was born, African, yet American."

Reverend Brown wiped his brow. "And just as the Lord kept his promise to the oppressed Israelites, we know that our Lord Jesus Christ has extended his mercy to his suffering black children."

"This is the meaning of Juneteenth. Freedom. On this date, a new black man was born in America." He raised his finger in warning. "But this did not mean the end of our struggle. Oh no. We had to strive for another hundred years for the Civil Rights movement, to fight against discrimination, segregation and Jim Crow. And the fight continues to this day!"

Reverend Brown remained silent for a minute, standing in somber attention. "Let us pray," he said finally. The congregation stood up and lowered their eyes. Chantley followed their example.

"Father, I stretch my hand to Thee—for no other help I know. Oh, my Rose of Sharon, my shelter in the time of storm. My Prince of Peace, my hope in this harsh land. We bow before You this morning to thank You for watching over us and taking care of us. This morning You touched us and brought us out of the land of slumber, gave us another day—thank You, Jesus. We realize that many that talked as we now talk, this morning when their names were called, they failed to answer. Their voices were hushed up in death. Their souls had taken a flight and gone back to the God that gave it, but not so with us. We are thankful the sheet we covered with was not our winding-sheet, and the bed we slept on was not our cooling board. You spared us and gave us one more chance to pray. And Father, before we go further, we want to pause and thank You for forgiving our sins. Forgive all our wrongdoings. We don't deserve it, but You lengthened out the briskly threads of our lives and gave us another chance to pray, and Lord, for this, we thank You. Now Lord, when I've come to the end of my journey, when my praying days are done and time for me shall be no more; when these knees have bowed for the last time, when I too, like all others, must come in off the battlefield of life, when I'm through being 'buked and scorned, I pray for a home in glory.

"When I come down to the river of Jordan, hold the river still and let your servant cross over during a calm down. Father, I'll be looking for that land where Job said the wicked would cease from troubling us and our weary souls would be at rest; over there, where a thousand years is but a day in eternity, where I'll meet with loved ones and where I can sing praises to Thee, and we can say with the saints of old, Free at Last, Free at Last, thank God almighty, I am free at last. Your servant's prayer for Christ's sake. Amen!"

The congregation of the Missionary Baptist Church rose and clapped hands. Some church members went over to congratulate their pastor, while others set the table for the picnic.

The lady who had invited them to sit down introduced herself. "I'm Sister Joan. Who are you?"

"I'm Sam, and this is Chantley. We've come from Colorado."

"Colorado!" exclaimed Sister Joan. She eyed Chantley curiously. "You mean you've traveled with this white girl all the way down here?"

Sam smiled. "Yes, ma'am,"

She shook her head. "Lord have mercy. All I know is that white girls with black men mostly cause trouble."

Chantley turned red. "But I like dark-skinned men!"

Sister Joan peered at her over her glasses. "I'm sure you do." She turned her attention to Sam. "Many of these white girls nowadays take to our black men."

Sam laughed. "Look. I know what you're saying," he said, "but this is the twenty-first century, not the nineteen-forties."

"You might think things have changed," answered Sister Joan, "but some folks haven't, especially around here."

Sam nodded his head. "I'll keep that in mind."

Sister Joan glanced at them doubtfully. "Come, try our food. I baked three trays of cornbread myself."

Chapter Twenty-two

In addition to waking late the next morning, not to mention a lazy lunch at an Indian restaurant that Chantley insisted on visiting, a traffic jam on the way out of Houston resulted in an inordinate delay. By the time they reached the city's eastern outskirts, it was well past three in the afternoon. "Shall we just spend another day here?" asked Chantley.

"No," said Sam. "I want to return to the Interstate as soon as possible."

Two and a half hours later, they crossed the border into Louisiana. "It felt like we drove through Texas forever," Chantley remarked.

The land displayed its own charms—flat, dotted with water bodies and densely populated with palms, cypress, and mangrove. The highway wound through miles of thick swamp and skirted muddy bayous. The salt from the sea, never far away, tingled in Chantley's nose.

An hour past the state border, the rain, which had threatened all day, finally opened up, and a monsoon thundered down, slowing their progress to a crawl.

"Shall we stop for the night?" questioned Chantley. "It's seven and already dark." The combination of twilight, low dark clouds and the rain sweeping in from the sea in blinding sheets dropped the visibility dangerously.

"I hoped to drive most of the night." Sam glanced at her and smiled sheepishly. "Never mind, let's stop at the next motel."

They took the next exit, and a roadside motel—about twenty cabins set a hundred feet from the road, framed by a dense green thicket—showed up a couple of miles later.

"How about this place?" asked Sam.

"It looks kind of deserted, doesn't it?" asked Chantley. She caught herself. "Sure, why not?"

They parked the car and, getting drenched, ran into the closest cabin, which sported a red neon "OPEN" sign in the front window.

A shabby green sofa sat next to the entrance of the small front room while a counter ran along its opposite wall. Behind it, on the wall, hung the stuffed head of an enormous dark-brown feral pig with tusks on both the upper and lower jaws, while sounds of a football game wafted in from a door situated on the far left. Chantley realized that the owner lived there. It must get pretty lonely, she thought. Sam pushed a buzzer on the counter, and a minute later, a burly middle-aged man appeared, stuffing his shirt into his pants. A thick brown mustache curled around his upper lips. He rubbed his bloodshot eyes and glanced at them momentarily. Chantley's gut tightened. The man was drunk.

He began silently arranging things on the counter. Chantley felt no friendliness from the man. His face appeared expressionless, and his manner was brusque. "What do you want?" he asked, not looking up.

"We're looking for a room for the night," replied Sam.

"One room?"

"Yes," replied Chantley.

The man slammed a drawer shut and swore. He stared at Sam. "What's a nigger like you doing with this white girl here?"

The situation alarmed Chantley. She clutched Sam's arm, feeling his muscles tense.

The motel owner glared at her. "How much money is he giving you?'

"What do you mean?' asked Chantley.

"I run a respectable establishment. I don't cater to people like you."

Sam flushed. "Hey, it's nothing like that," he protested loudly. "We're just traveling together."

"Where you two from?" questioned the man.

"Colorado," answered Chantley, her heart pounding.

"This here ain't no Colorado."

Perplexed, she knotted her eyebrows.

"Let me tell you something. Here, folks respect each other. We don't cotton to black men out at night with white women."

"Hey," yelled Sam. "How's that any of your business?"

Alarm bells went off in Chantley's head. She stepped back, still holding Sam's arm.

The man opened a swing gate at the right end of the counter and walked out in front. "You just asking for trouble, aren't you?"

Chantley fear turned into panic. "Let's leave!" she whispered, but Sam clenched his hands, ready for an altercation.

"How 'bout I kick your ass from here to Texas?" he questioned.

"You better get the hell out," said the man, "before I go back and get my shotgun."

"Please," pleaded Chantley, her hands shaking. "Please stop this!"

Sam glared at the man. Chantley felt Sam's pulse pounding in his arms. "Please! Let's leave."

"That's right, nigger. Just leave. You're in my town and in my place."

Sam took a step back and kicked the sofa with all his might. It skated across the floor and smashed into the wall.

"That's it, you bastard," yelled the man. "I'm getting my gun." He stomped back through the swing gate.

Chantley desperately pulled at Sam, her face white, her hands trembling. Sam took a deep breath, spun around and strode out the door.

*****

Sam drove off angrily, swooping and swerving in the dark and the rain, not speaking. Chantley kept quiet. She understood him well enough to know when to comfort him and when to wait. An electric current of anxiety raced through her body, and her hands trembled. She closed her eyes and concentrated on her breathing, allowing herself to calm down.

After twenty minutes of screeching tires outside and absolute silence inside, they came to a level crossing. Sam pulled to the side of the road, turned off the engine and sat silently, listening to the drumbeat of the rain pounding the automobile's roof. She had been wise to wait. Sam's face no longer contorted with rage; in fact, he looked contemplative.

"I feel sorry for that guy," he said.

His reaction astonished Chantley. "Why?"

"Racist people came from conflicted families. Study after study proves that. It's a reaction to frustrations suffered inside the family environment." He glanced at her. "You know what a scapegoat is?"

"The projecting of weakness onto others?"

"Exactly. The same family situations produce hatred of Blacks, Jews, Catholics and others."

"You feel sorry for him because of that?'

"People are not born with hate. It has to be imprinted and constantly fostered. Racists not only victimize others, but they're also victims of their environment."

Sam raised his eyes and peered into the rain. "Honestly, it's not the fight for equal rights or the right to vote that white people fear. It's myths like all black men are sexually rapacious that are at fault. It's this element of sexuality, this notion of racial purity—that black men pollute white women—that's at the root of racial prejudice in America."

Chantley ran her fingers through her hair. It's the same in many parts of the world, she thought. Almost everywhere, men think they own women. They call it 'honor,' and for that, women get raped and killed. Women's bodies are seen as repositories of privilege for the dominating class, and power and ownership are expressed by controlling them.

She remembered her history classes. During the liberation of Bangladesh, the oppressing Pakistani forces stated their supremacy by raping over two hundred thousand women. They did this for two reasons: to humiliate the Bengalis, as if to say, 'we can do what we want to your women, and you can't do anything about it,' and secondly, by that physical act, to convey their ability to dominate an entire nation.

"And there are no consequences when it's done the other way," said Sam.

"In which way?"

"Ownership of female slaves included any sexual contact that owners desired. While sexual attention directed at white women attracts serious repercussions, white sexuality directed at black women had no consequences." Sam shook his head sadly. "If America is a person, and you put it on a psychiatrist's couch, the diagnosis would be a split personality."

Chantley gazed at him quizzically.

"It means having multiple identities in the same person. America is like that: having different people with different histories and cultures occupying the same body. And when one identity conflicts with another, violence boils over."

Sam looked resigned and hopeless. Chantley reached over and held his hand, kneading his disappointments until his melancholy disappeared. He smiled. He pulled her over and kissed her. Outside, on the railroad tracks, the whistle of an approaching freight train sounded long in the night, and, in a rush of power and passion, it thundered by for uncountable minutes. Chantley felt incredibly in the moment, yet floating far above in space, and their kiss ended only when the rhythmic thumping of the boxcars on the steel tracks disappeared into the distance.

"Wow!" he said.

She gasped. For several minutes she sat still, composing herself. She suddenly noticed something. "Listen," she said.

"What?"

"Do you hear that?"

Sam scratched his head. "I don't hear a thing."

"Exactly. The rain has stopped." She opened the window and cool, humid night air flowed into the car's muggy interior. She breathed deeply and calmed her pounding heart.

Sam turned on the car engine. "Let's go."

Chapter Twenty-three

Their walk in downtown New Orleans ended at St. Louis Cathedral at Jackson Square. The small park, enclosed by an iron railing, didn't impress, but the Cathedral, large and massively constructed, with three black spires jutting into the sky, certainly made an impact. Sam stopped and looked around as Chantley eyed him enquiringly.

"There," he exclaimed, walking towards a bronze statue of a man astride a horse holding his hat in hand. Chantley followed and saw, to her surprise, a familiar, tall, clean-shaven man, one she had met at the end-of-school picnic in the hills near Boulder.

"DeAngelo," shouted Sam, ran over and gave him a bear hug.

"Welcome to my town!" said DeAngelo.

"This is Lakeisha," said DeAngelo, introducing his girlfriend, who, in turn, embraced Chantley. Lakeisha looked stunning in her leopard-print dress and her understated but expert makeup. She stood slim and tall, at least four inches taller than Chantley, and her red high heels made her tower over her.

"Chantley, right?" DeAngelo asked, turning his attention to her, regarding her curiously. He glanced at Sam. "You two are kind of serious, aren't you?"

Sam smiled. "I guess you could say that." Chantley nodded her head.

Lakeisha stepped in. "Chantley. What a sweet name!" She grabbed her right hand. "And you're so pretty!" Chantley blushed.

"How about we sit down and talk?" asked Sam.

"Sure," said DeAngelo. "Let's go to the Cafe du Monde. It's close by, and on the way, we'll explore the French Quarter."

Lakeisha turned tourist guide, pointing out the city's architecture and recounting its history. New Orleans resembled no city Chantley had visited. She felt its age in her bones, a city that kept drowning and rebuilding itself over the centuries. Catholic cathedrals, art galleries, and museums lined its streets. Long, narrow Shotgun houses, painted in colorful pastels, pushed up against each other while large iconic Creole townhouses featuring intricate ironwork balconies touched the sidewalks.

The buildings in the French Quarter, primarily single-story Creole cottages with steeply pitched roofs and small porches in front, dated back a hundred and fifty years, with many much older. Impatient, New Orleans could not sit still. The narrow streets brought an intimate feel to the neighborhood while the restless street life spouted a never-ending energy.

New Orleans constituted an ongoing competition: some houses old and crumbling while renovations continued unabated on others; the dredgers on the Mississippi constantly sucking up mud and flushing it further downstream; traditional Cajun and Zydeco music squaring off against mellifluous Jazz melodies; Acadian French coexisting uneasily with modern American idiom. Waves of cultures and languages—French, Spanish, American, White, Creole and Black—rolled in and out of the city like the Gulf tide. This never-ending tug-of-war between nature and humanity; old and new; one culture and another, and between the different races defined the land and its people.

They reached the restaurant, occupied a table under the awning, and ordered sodas while a three-man band played cool jazz.

"How's that internship?" asked Sam.

"Good," replied DeAngelo. "I work for the city as a junior engineer in the Stormwater Management and Green Infrastructure Department. It keeps the city drained and constructs buildings and plants related to water management. It's really important here."

"Where are you headed to?" asked Lakeisha.

"Charleston," replied Sam.

"Why?" asked DeAngelo.

"To learn a bit about myself; where I came from."

DeAngelo rubbed his chin, puzzled.

Sam listed the facts discovered during the regression and his research. "After everything, I had to check it out."

DeAngelo nodded his head. "You've always been interested in slave times. So, I'm not surprised."

Lakeisha turned to Chantley. "What brought you along?"

"I planned to go east anyhow to find my mother." She briefly recounted her journey from India. After Charleston, she would travel to Pittsburgh. A sharp anxiety arose in her chest. Her mother had escaped her mind the past few days. *Where would I stay? How can I locate my mother?* She pushed the thoughts away. Being with Sam calmed her; stopped her from falling into a panic.

"When Sam invited me to join him, I agreed," she said. "Crossing the country by myself didn't appeal to me. And it saved me a good bit of money."

"I don't believe you!" exclaimed Lakeisha.

"What do you mean?"

"Both of you are being so rational, giving all kinds of reasons that make sense."

Chantley's mind went blank.

"You can't fool me," declared Lakeisha. "You like each other a lot, don't you?" DeAngelo burst out laughing.

"Of course we do," admitted Sam, winking at Chantley.

Chantley glanced at Sam. "Sam and I want to find out if we had a relationship in the past." She averted her eyes. "After that, who knows?"

"This is just like one of those romances, isn't it?" exclaimed Lakeisha. "The ones you read about in books!"

Chantley turned red. 'I don't know about that," she mumbled.

"I have an idea," said Lakeisha as they finished their cold drinks. "Why don't we let the guys spend some time together while we do some girl stuff?"

DeAngelo agreed. "Go ahead. It'll give Sam and me a chance to catch up. How about we meet back in front of the Cathedral in a couple of hours?"

Lakeisha grabbed Chantley's arm. "Let's go!"

Chantley got up. "What do you suggest?"

"How about we shop for clothes?" Chantley brightened up, tired of living out of a suitcase and repeatedly wearing the same things. "What's available around here?"

"Everything you can think of and a few you can't imagine!"

Chantley laughed. She liked Lakeisha's bubbly nature and infectious smile, not to mention the opportunity for female companionship.

"Visitors usually end up here in the French Quarter, paying double," added Lakeisha. "I know exactly where to shop!"

They caught the Uptown bus to Tulane University, where Lakeisha attended classes, and wandered through streets lined with palm, oak, and myrtle. "We get the funkiest fashion here," said Lakeisha.

"Really?"

"Yeah, and the prices are just right."

They entered a basement shop filled with wildly-colored blouses, slacks and dresses, all cut to the latest fashion. After an hour of strolling in and out of at least a dozen shops, Chantley's sole purchase amounted to a pair of jeans, while Lakeisha carried two full shopping bags.

"How about we grab a coffee before heading back?"

"Sure."

They walked into a specialty beignet shop, bought their coffees and sat on the patio under a canvas canopy. A breeze blew in from across the Mississippi, relieving the muggy day. Chantley felt a tremor of delight. "I love the weather here!"

"It's not for everyone. Northerners come here in the fall and winter, but the summers are too hot for them." She looked keenly at Chantley. "DeAngelo has told me a lot about Sam, but he's never mentioned you. Have you known each other for some time?"

"Only for maybe a month and a half."

"No way!" Lakeisha smiled mischievously. "You must really like each other."

Chantley nodded her head. "Yes, we do."

"Tell me everything! Where did you meet? How did you hit it off so quickly?" Lakeisha's eyes sparkled with excitement and curiosity.

"Sam was sitting on a bench reading a book. The first time I looked into his eyes, I felt a shock of electricity go through me."

"Oh, my, my!" Lakeisha bubbled. "How romantic! How wonderful! Love at first sight!"

Chantley caught Lakeisha's excitement. "Yes! I guess you could say that."

"I've always wondered how that would feel. I've known DeAngelo for years, but we still haven't figured out where we're going."

"I'm not sure Sam and I have figured it out either."

"Why not? I always thought that once you fall in love, I mean truly in love, it's forever."

"I do love Sam," replied Chantley. "But I'm not sure about committing just yet."

Lakeisha leaned over and patted Chantley's hands. "Of course. You want to be sure."

Chantley nodded, glad to have Lakeisha to talk to about her relationship. *That's what I've been missing: another woman to talk to about my feelings.* "I guess I should just go ahead and make a commitment."

Lakeisha clapped her hands. "There you go. You're so pretty, and he's so good-looking. You make a perfect pair!"

Chantley felt her doubts and misgivings disappear. Yes, Sam was meant for her. "But it's up to him too, isn't it?"

"Sure," replied Lakeisha, with a twinkle in her eyes.

*****

Back at the French Quarter, DeAngelo invited Sam and Chantley to their place. "How long are you staying in New Orleans?" he asked.

"Leaving tomorrow morning," replied Sam.

"No way," interrupted Lakeisha. "You guys can't leave just like that. Take a little break. Spend a few days with us."

Chantley nodded her head. What a welcome invitation! *I'm just becoming friends with Lakeisha.*

"I don't know," started Sam.

"Hey man, what's the problem?" asked DeAngelo. "You're my brother from university. The first one to visit me. You can't just leave like that."

"I've got to be careful with the money," mumbled Sam.

Lakeisha interrupted. "But if you stay with us, it will not cost you a penny."

Sam still hesitated. He kept his eyes on the ground. Lakeisha looked at Chantley as if to say, 'How come you're not speaking up?'

"I think it's a great idea," exclaimed Chantley. Sam frowned. His reaction caught her off guard. *Is he upset? Is it so important to get back on the road?*

DeAngelo took her words for assent. "It's settled. I'll take a few days off work, and we'll spend the time together."

*****

Chantley hardly saw Sam the next day. The men went off while she and Lakeisha spent the day exploring the city. Lakeisha had relaxed her hair, tied it with a bright blue ribbon and wore an impossibly-tight ivory blouse with a short lilac skirt with black pumps. A large black belt circled her thin, tight waist, and her constant smile, which lit up her face, dazzled Chantley. She admired Lakeisha's fashion sense, though she admitted she couldn't pull it off. To look and dress like Lakeisha required not just flair but also immense confidence.

Lakeisha took her to a basement jazz club in the historic Treme district, where she sang on Friday nights and the weekends. Chantley felt as if entering a cool dark cave. The place was surprisingly large, and the staff greeted Lakeisha warmly. In the afternoon, the place was almost empty.

"That's where I perform," she said, pointing to a slightly raised stage near the back.

"There is so much music here," exclaimed Chantley, the sounds of omnipresent street musicians still sounding in her ears. They sat down.

"You're in such good shape," stated Lakeisha, admiring Chantley. "How do you keep your figure?"

"I practice yoga. I've been teaching it for the past few years."

"No way! I've thought about it myself but never got around to doing it."

"I'd love to teach you," offered Chantley.

"You don't have to!"

"I insist." Chantley glanced at her friend. "For me, it's not just a way of keeping in shape. Yoga gives a feeling of peacefulness and contentment that I don't think you can get anywhere else. It connects me to the spirit. If more people practiced yoga, we'd have less violence. Teaching is a way of giving back, of helping the world."

"I'll take you up on the offer," said Lakeisha. "I'm so hyper all the time. Peacefulness is just what I need!"

Chantley spent the rest of the day and the next few browsing, sightseeing, and shopping, returning to her friends' condominium late each evening. The apartment, designed in an open style, had a small modern kitchen, a large dining area for a table and four chairs, two bedrooms and a spacious sunken living room. Chantley caught her friend's excitement for clothing and returned each evening with purchases, collapsing on the sofa in the living room. Sam usually sat on a loveseat, watching television. He would say nothing, but she noticed him looking disapprovingly at the shopping bags.

His reaction caught her off guard. *Why would he be bothered? It's my money.* Ever since their arrival in New Orleans, Sam had been distant. On one hand, he thoroughly enjoyed being with his friends. Still, on the other, he displayed a growing restlessness and impatience with each passing day, dropping hints of his contradictory moods with glances and silences. Chantley frowned and bit her lip. His behavior irritated her.

The next day, Chantley prepared lunch. Indian, of course, was the only cuisine in which she showed proficiency. Excited to cook for her new friends, she had woken early, shopped, and wore a favorite new outfit—a bright red pleated skirt that Lakeisha insisted suited her perfectly. It differed from the ordinary, pale colors of the rest of her wardrobe. She paired it with a long-sleeve ivory blouse.

It took a couple of hours, and Chantley had three hungry customers. First came the appetizer—fresh okra sliced in halves, coated with a slightly salted and mildly spiced chickpea batter, and deep fried until golden. The contrast between the crunch of the exterior and the softness of the vegetable made the dish delectable.

As they crowded the small dinner table, she rushed in from the kitchen with a plate of piping hot chapattis—unleavened whole-wheat bread—cooked on the stovetop. She served it with chard, shredded, slow-cooked with fava beans and carrots, spiced with classic hot Cajun seasoning and cane sugar, giving the slightly bitter leaves a pleasing touch of heat and sweetness.

The next dish, a Louisiana classic, came from a recipe from Lakeisha: red beans cooked with celery, bell pepper and onions with Cajun spices, served over brown rice. The hearty dish left everyone satisfied. Dessert consisted of plain yogurt served over sliced red and yellow figs, with a spoon of honey on top. DeAngelo went for seconds.

"This is satisfying," he remarked. "Thank you." The others expressed their appreciation. Chantley beamed.

The diners leaned back, satiated, as Chantley cleared the table. As she picked up the pot containing the chard, it slipped from her hand, depositing the contents on her skirt. The liquid and the beans slid down and dropped on the floor, leaving a large stain on the red fabric.

"Oh no!" she exclaimed.

Lakeisha rushed over with a wet towel and rubbed the skirt. It didn't help. "I'm afraid it won't come out," she remarked.

"That's what you get for wasting your money," said Sam, frowning.

Chantley's eyes widened. His poor mood finally burst into the open. "It's been building for a few days, hasn't it?" she hissed. "What's bothering you?"

"You don't understand how things work in this world. I've noticed you're spending money like there's no tomorrow."

"You think I'm stupid, don't you?" she retorted. "You couldn't care if I'm happy or not." She slammed the pot on the table. Sam glowered.

Lakeisha intervened. Rubbing Chantley's arm, she guided her to the seat next to her. "You've told us about growing up in India, but you never mentioned that you're such a good cook!" said Lakeisha in an apparent attempt to normalize the situation. "And life in a foreign country? You must have had so many adventures."

"Yes, but it was home. I never felt alone, despite having almost no family there," Chantley replied, her head hung low.

"Her Dad passed away a few years back," explained Sam. "He was a hippie who wandered all over. Maybe he didn't know what to do with his life."

Chantley's eyes widened. What an unexpected and uncaring thing to say! Her father never behaved irresponsibly. He spent his life taking care of others; if not her, then the visitors to the ashram. He loved her, loved her madly, and the bond between them remained inseparable.

"At least my dad didn't leave me," she snapped. As soon as she said it, she regretted it. It was a sensitive topic for Sam. He always mentioned his mother and grandmother affectionately but avoided talk of his father.

"I didn't mean to criticize your father," he retorted.

Chantley could not hold back. "You are such a jerk," she yelled.

Lakeisha looked at her wide-eyed.

"What about your mother?" asked DeAngelo, quickly changing the topic.

"My mom left when I was just a kid," she replied, not looking up.

Sam huffed. "I can't imagine anyone doing that," he said, almost flippantly. His comment cut Chantley to the core. Despite everything, she knew that her mother loved her. That was why she'd come to America, to reconnect and join the only one left of her family. Things could seem so different from the outside. Not every young woman is ready for motherhood—her mother had her demons to battle. But she never disliked Chantley.

"From what I've seen, my family is better than yours," she mumbled. "Looks like your Mom gave birth to a loser."

Sam put his fork down. "Who gives birth to a kid in a foreign country and leaves her there? Come on, can't you see that? Don't you realize she was at least a bit immature?" A shocked silence fell on the small group.

"What's the matter with you?" Chantley's temper flared. She had never thought of her mother that way. Both hurt and defiant, her fingers shook, and her face flushed. Finally, she slammed her hand on the table. "You're nasty. I can't stand you!"

"That's what I get for trusting a white woman," he hissed.

Chantley trembled. Is this what I came to America? Did I leave my father's grave for this? Hot, burning tears streamed down her face.

"Oh my," exclaimed Lakeisha, running over. "Chantley, don't cry!'

Burning with humiliation, stung with shame, Chantley bawled. Stumbling, she got up and ran into her room, leaving Lakeisha stunned, DeAngelo alarmed, and Sam gazing sheepishly at the floor.

Chapter Twenty-four

Sam looked out over the Mississippi. Its turbidity mirrored his feelings. He spent the day wandering the French Quarter, taking the ferry across the river to Algiers Point, returned for lunch at Decatur Street and now, in the late afternoon, met his friend at the Riverwalk.

"What'up?" asked DeAngelo. His workplace was just a few blocks away, and he was dressed in business formal wear—suit and tie—and carried his briefcase in hand. "You wanna talk?"

Sam did, but his mind felt heavy and listless. Was this the end with Chantley? Would he continue to South Carolina by himself? Without her, the trip threatened to be meaningless. He shook his head and concentrated. "Yes, but I don't know where to start."

"Do you love Chantley?"

"Absolutely."

"So, what happened last night?"

"I didn't mean to criticize her father. She described him as a hippie, and I just repeated it. She reacted very emotionally to something factual."

"You criticized her mother." DeAngelo shook his head. "That's a big no-no."

"I guess," said Sam. "But only after she brought up my father." He looked at DeAngelo. "She said some mean things about my mother; about me."

"And what did you mean about her being white?"

Sam looked down. "I snapped. I regret saying that. I used to feel that way when I was younger. It's an attitude I got from my grandma."

"What else is going on?"

Sam scratched his forehead. "I worry about her. She's been so sheltered and knows nothing about America. She misunderstands things. Like I'm trying to warn her about her finances, but she thinks I'm trying to make her unhappy. Neither one of us knows where the other is coming from."

"Anything else?"

"She's really sensitive. She gets hurt quickly and retreats. Then it becomes difficult to communicate." He looked at his friend. "You think I'm a bad person?"

"No," assured his friend. "You're a good man."

"What should I do? How can I make it up to her?"

DeAngelo glanced away hesitantly.

"Come on," prodded Sam.

"I don't want you to take this the wrong way."

"What is it?"

DeAngelo sighed. "You're my brother, so I'll be honest with you. Often, you can be hard to relate to. You got philosophy and history on your brain all the time."

"No, I don't," protested Sam.

DeAngelo shook his head. "Sometimes you've got your head so wrapped up in your thoughts that you don't pay attention to people."

"I never meant..."

DeAngelo interrupted. "Of course not, but I'll repeat it. Sometimes your attitude can be intimidating."

Sam had to admit he could be a bit distant at times. His mother had told him the same thing: that he differed from everyone in his family. "Chantley's also hard to understand."

"What do you mean?"

"She has a different way of looking at the world. For example, she thinks we have a karmic relationship."

"What's the problem with that?"

"I'm hesitant to accept it."

DeAngelo glanced at him with round eyes and raised eyebrows.

"First, I don't understand all its implications and consequences. Second, I need proof. I can't accept a belief even if deeply felt."

"But isn't this what your travel to South Carolina is all about? To find out if it's real?"

"You're right," admitted Sam. "What should I do?"

DeAngelo looked out at the river. "Do you try to understand her way of thinking?"

Sam rubbed his forehead, perplexed.

DeAngelo sighed. "I get it. This is a communication problem. Speak in a way she understands."

"You're asking me to change my way of thinking?"

"No," answered DeAngelo. "Even if you don't accept her point of view, try to understand it. It's important to her."

Sam had to admit that DeAngelo's logic made sense. He did approach things intellectually. After all, DeAngelo was one of the most level-headed, practical persons he knew. And he got along well with Lakeisha.

"Look at this way," continued DeAngelo. "You just might discover a new way of looking at things."

"Fine. I'll try my best."

"It's all related to what I said. Have you done anything special with her? Did you buy her anything meaningful?"

"I've taken care of expenses."

DeAngelo laughed. "It's obvious you don't know much about women. You told me this is your first real relationship, and you don't know how to handle it."

"True," admitted Sam. "Chantley is the first girl I've ever deeply loved." Is my lack of experience with romance this obvious? He looked at his friend hopefully. "How can I mend fences with Chantley?"

"Roses, jewelry, chocolates, nice restaurants. Women love that kind of stuff. If I were you, I'd be treating my woman every day. Apologize to her and open up. Be more understanding."

"That's it?"

"Absolutely. Instead of being so serious, be in the moment. Have fun. Pay attention to her. She'll love it!"

Sam laughed. "Okay. Got it."

*****

Chantley spent most of the next day sitting alone in the condominium, not eating and moping around absent-mindedly. DeAngelo returned to work, and Lakeisha attended classes while Sam disappeared, probably not wanting to face her. The insecurity and unease of her initial days in America returned full force, and a sense of abandonment filled her heart. She felt betrayed by Sam.

At the precise moment their relationship gathered momentum, he had knocked it off its moorings.

What will I do now? I'll have to catch a bus to Pittsburgh. She stuffed her clothes into her suitcase but felt too overwhelmed to make an immediate move. The thoughts of her mother brought no solace. *What will I say when I meet her?*

Lakeisha returned at four o'clock. "How are you doing?" she asked. Chantley forced a smile and hesitantly nodded. Lakeisha noticed the open suitcase and shook her head gravely. "Why don't we get something to eat? DeAngelo has Sam staying over at a friend's place tonight. It will give us a chance to talk."

For the first time that day, Chantley smiled. *Thank God for Lakeisha. At least I have her.* And she discovered that, indeed, she felt ravenous. "Let's go," she replied.

*****

Chantley silently ate her po-boy, a crusty French baguette slathered with a tangy, creamy remoulade, stuffed with breaded, fried mushrooms and 'slaw, her appetite superseding conversation. Finally, over apple pie and whipped cream, she opened up. "I don't know what to do. I don't see how I can trust Sam again."

Lakeisha nodded her head understandingly. "What do you mean?"

200

"What he said about my parents hurt." Her eyes moistened.

Lakeisha eyed Chantley keenly. "You're right. That was a cruel thing to say. So what are you going to do?"

"I still have options. I can catch a bus to Pittsburgh. That was my original plan anyway."

"You sure you want to do that?"

"I have to admit I'm unsure about this relationship. I wonder what I got myself into. Is this what he's actually like?"

Lakeisha waited for Chantley to continue.

"And what did he mean about not trusting white women?"

Lakeisha arched her eyebrows and looked away, avoiding the issue.

"Sam has two sides: one, generous and caring while the other, inconsiderate and controlling," complained Chantley, "as if everything revolves around him and I didn't count for anything. I noticed he gets upset when I spend money on myself. And what he said yesterday—as if he was jealous of me for having parents who love me." It baffled and infuriated her. She cared for and loved him, but his behavior couldn't help to raise doubts.

"You're right."

"How about my feelings? Don't my opinions count for anything? I thought of Sam as my protector. I trusted him fully. Why did he mess everything up?"

A sudden fear arose in her chest. *Am I clinging to Sam because of my vulnerability and fear? Am I being desperate? Am I ignoring warning signs?*

"Men can be such jerks," said Lakeisha sympathetically.

"It came so suddenly. Why did he fight with me?"

Lakeisha raised her left eyebrow. "You fought with each other."

That's true; I did comment on his father.

"Also, the moment I laid eyes on you, I could tell you're the sensitive type."

Chantley rubbed her chin. "I guess. If he said something about me, it would be different. But to insult my Mom and Dad? That crossed the line."

"You tell me which man out there is thoughtful about a woman's feelings?" Lakeisha waved her hands as if dismissing something trivial. "I've known a lot of men—some bad. I don't see Sam being one. Maybe Sam had a bad night. He's a good man, at least from what DeAngelo told me. But at the same time, I understand your position."

Chantley glanced out the restaurant's window. Was Lakeisha right? Had she judged Sam too harshly? True, she'd been pretty sensitive ever since Vijay broke her heart.

Lakeisha leaned over and whispered, "You're kind of inexperienced around men, aren't you?"

Chantley blushed. "You're right." She hesitated and then admitted. "There was someone."

Lakeisha immediately interrupted. "And you're still in love with him?"

"No. It ended."

Lakeisha shook her head. "It might be over, but maybe you haven't put it behind you?"

"It's dead now." Chantley sighed. "It never had a chance."

Her friend nodded her head. "Good. Carrying things like that can be torture." She reached over and touched Chantley's hand. "Let me suggest something before you pack up and head out of town."

"What's that?"

"Talk with Sam. See what he has to say."

*****

"Come in," said DeAngelo. Sam hesitated for a moment as he stood at the front door, hat in hand, before striding in.

Chantley, sitting at the dining table, stiffened and looked at the floor as DeAngelo walked Sam over.

"You guys go ahead," said DeAngelo as he moved over to the living room and joined Lakeisha, who sat watching a television program with the volume turned up to provide them a little privacy.

Sam sat on a chair opposite Chantley. "I wasn't thinking," he started.

Chantley said nothing. Sam tried again. "I'm sorry; I didn't mean to hurt your feelings. I didn't think when I spoke about your parents."

Chantley shook her head. "I feel you've been upset with me for the past few days."

"I guess," conceded Sam.

"Why is that?'

"I wanted to be careful with the money."

"But those were my purchases."

"I didn't expect to stay in New Orleans for long, and we've been here for almost a week. Even if we're staying here with DeAngelo, the expenses add up. So I want to keep within my budget for this trip. And seeing you with all those new clothes, I guess, got me disturbed."

"But it doesn't make any sense. It's my money."

Sam rubbed his forehead. "I grew up poor. We never spent money on anything except the necessities."

"I didn't grow up with much either," she countered. "But I never lived in anxiety. Why are you always worried about money? Why can't you be pleased with whatever comes your way?"

"I understand your point, but it's different. Even if you grew up poor, you didn't grow up rough. From what you tell me, you grew up in a community that gave you a lot of support. I grew up fending for myself, learning many lessons on who to trust and, mostly, who not to trust. We had gangs and violence—stuff you never dealt with."

"It seems very domineering."

Sam struggled. "I'm sorry it came out that way. I was trying to warn you that you'll be in for a rough ride if you don't take care of your money."

"But did you have to be so cruel?" She had never fought with Vijay; never had an unpleasant word passed between them. Now, she had to deal with an insensitive man she had no idea how to handle. "This is not the first time you've been inconsiderate. That's what concerns me. Is this a pattern?"

"It's not like that at all," protested Sam. "You're taking this the wrong way."

Chantley sat glumly. She was venting her frustrations, and Sam was becoming defensive. Sam gazed restlessly at the ceiling. It wasn't working for him either. Chantley kept silent for a moment, gathering the courage to continue the conversation. "You said something about not trusting white women. It shocked me. What did you mean?"

"When you mentioned my dad, it made me angry." He shifted in his seat. "I didn't mean to say that."

"But you did. It had to come from somewhere."

Sam took a deep breath. "It starts with my grandfather."

She looked at him quizzically.

"My grandmother married a white man," he mumbled.

"You told me once."

"I don't like talking about him."

"Why?"

"He caused a lot of damage to my family. He left after five years and never returned. But not before he fathered four kids. One of them was my father, who, in turn, left my mother. Because of him, I distrust white people."

"You're upset because he abandoned her?"

"It's more than that," replied Sam.

"What do you mean?"

"Because of him, I have white blood in my veins."

Chantley shot a look at Sam's eyes. They looked blank, and the turmoil behind them distant but evident. This explains his moodiness! Sam's self-conception was that of a proud black man. Did this bit of white ancestry gall him?

"I feel like one part of me is fighting the other." He glanced at her, and she saw in his eyes, for a moment, a glimpse of his vulnerability. "I guess that's why I have all these questions. I ask myself who I am. What part of me belongs where?"

He looked away. The moment of opening departed as quickly as it had arrived. *His pride won't let him continue, but I'm grateful he revealed this much.* They sat awkwardly for a while, each gazing at the ceiling in opposite directions.

Sam pulled out something from his pocket. "I didn't know what to get you, but here's a gift."

A chocolate heart sat inside a yellow box about three inches on each side, with a red bow stuck on top. She had to suppress a smile. As if this silly piece of chocolate would fix everything. A typical male thing, precisely what she expected Sam to do. But she gave him credit for trying.

"What now?" he asked.

She glanced at him, not unkindly. "Give me one more day to think about this. I'd appreciate it."

Sam got up and, without saying a word, left.

Chapter Twenty-five

The Voudon priestess wore a white dress reaching her ankles, a bleached sleeveless cotton blouse and a white lace bandana tying her hair back. She sat on an oversized chair—a throne, really—in the middle of a large room occupying the ground floor of a Shotgun house in the historic Faubourg Marigny district, with its stucco walls the color of ripe green melons. An incredible number of knick-knacks occupied the floor while African masks, portraits of the Virgin Mary, Tibetan Thankas and tie-dyed Hindu deities covered the walls. At its far end stood a wooden altar, crowded with an eclectic collection of religious figures and icons.

"What can I do for you?" asked the priestess. Despite her uncommon dress and the exotic setting, she looked far more prosaic with short-cropped gray hair, thick lenses set in large black frames and the weary, no-nonsense manner of someone's grandmother who had seen it all.

Chantley glanced hesitantly at Lakeisha.

"I brought her here," replied her friend. "She's going through a rough time."

"My name is Queen Josephine," said the lady, holding a solid but well-worn hand. "I'm the Mambo of this temple."

Chantley glanced at Lakeisha. "Mambo is the title for a Voudon priestess," explained her friend.

Queen Josephine glanced at Chantley. "So, you're having man problems?"

The comment took Chantley aback. How did she know? "Yes," she admitted. "Most of the time, he's nice..."

"But he doesn't treat you right, he doesn't respect you, he hurts your feelings."

Chantley's jaw dropped. "How did you know?"

The old lady rubbed her walnut-brown cheeks. "If I had a dime for every woman who complains to me about how her man treats her, I'd be sitting on a million dollars."

Chantley looked around, discombobulated. "I don't know anything about what you do."

"I can't tell you everything about Voudon in the time we have," replied Queen Josephine, "but I will tell you a bit."

Chantley nodded her head.

"Voudon comes from Africa," continued the old lady. "The trans-Atlantic slave trade brought West Africans, mostly Fon, Bambara and Mandinga, to America. Voudon is nothing more than the religious practices of the people of that region, still practiced by over thirty million West Africans to this day.

"Not just Americans and English engaged in the slave trade. The French also brought slaves from West Africa to their colonies in Haiti and Louisiana. According to French laws, unlike the English, slave children were not separated from their families at an early age, and many times, husbands and wives were not sold off separately. This allowed parents to teach the original African knowledge to their children. Voudon is not an organized religion. Unlike Western ones, where scripture is important, in Voudon, the personal spiritual power of the priest or priestess is paramount."

Chantley sat engrossed, listening. The similarities between African traditions and Hinduism were undoubtedly remarkable. She related it to the tradition of Gurus—those who transcended the dualities of the material world and whose spiritual attainments drew disciples to them.

"Voudon came to the Americas about three hundred years ago and, over time, certain aspects of French Catholicism merged with the original African beliefs to create Louisiana Voudon. And Haiti has its own version."

"That's interesting! Is it only practiced by the black community?"

"It has its roots in the African-American community, but you'd be surprised how many others have adopted it."

"There's a lot of misinformation about Voudon," added Lakeisha.

Queen Josephine nodded her head. "Most of that comes from Hollywood and popular novels, which label it a negative practice. And here in Louisiana, it has become somewhat commercialized."

"What is Voudon about?' asked Chantley.

"It's about healing. Allowing one to heal oneself. Not just the body—though we use a lot of herbs—but also curing the spirit."

"And how do you do that?"

"We perform rituals, we chant, do blessings and offer consultations." She pointed to rows of shelves built into the wall behind her, holding bottles filled with various liquids, small cloth bags stuffed with herbs and a vast array of charms. "These *gris-gris* are part of the healing also." She looked at Chantley. "What do you want to do?"

Chantley glanced at Lakeisha for help.

"How about a consultation?" suggested her friend.

Queen Josephine took off her glasses. "Sure. But don't just sit there expecting me to do all the work. I'll do the consulting, but you must exert yourself too."

Chantley nodded her head. She felt intimidated by the old lady's authority, yet Queen Josephine's confidence raised her hopes.

"Okay, tell me what's going on."

Chantley started describing her relationship with Sam, but Queen Josephine cut her off after a couple of minutes.

"You sure sound like a little lost bird."

The observation confounded Chantley. She felt as if she was being stared through. She opened her mouth but said nothing.

"Well?"

"I guess so." Chantley rubbed her forehead. "I'm new to this country." She lowered her eyes. "I'm all alone. I have no siblings, lost my father, and haven't seen my mother for maybe seventeen years."

Queen Josephine shook her head unsympathetically. "It doesn't matter. You find out what you're made of when you're tested." She sighed. "Have you always been this scared, this timid?"

"No," protested Chantley. "I've always been confident. It's only in the last couple of years when things started to go wrong, that my confidence took a beating. Especially…"

Queen Josephine cut her off. "The details aren't important." Chantley wanted so much to expose her feelings, about Vijay; about her father's death.

"It's when life turns against you that your real nature is revealed."

Chantley nodded her head hesitantly.

"I can tell you don't fully comprehend what I'm saying. You know the expression 'you create your own destiny'?"

Chantley's eyes widened. "Are you saying Sam behaves like he does because I'm letting him?"

Queen Josephine nodded her head gravely.

Chantley took a deep breath. Her vulnerability and loneliness certainly played a part in her reactions to situations. *Am I like this with Sam because of what happened with Vijay?*

The old lady peered at her over her glasses. "Sometimes, we make people react to us in certain ways without us even knowing it. Do you understand?"

"I think so. If I continue giving away my power, I'll keep attracting the same behavior from Sam or any other man."

"If you rediscover your confidence, maybe your relationship will change." She rubbed her cheeks. "I've been doing this for a long time, and I've learned that unequal relationships between men and women are never healthy. You need to treat each other as equals for your happiness, if not your man's."

Chantley remembered her father. As a child, she obeyed him while he, as a parent, was more powerful and in charge. But as she grew, the more equal their relationship became. Naturally progressing from dependency, growth had brought equality and latitude.

"The best relationships between men and women are equal ones. The love between adults not based on equality can never be completely satisfying."

Chantley nodded her head. Who doesn't want fulfilling relationships in their lives? But she had to rise above Sam's level of understanding and not be pulled into worry and fear by his actions.

Queen Josephine looked Chantley in the eyes. "You can't change circumstances, but you always have the power to react to them the way you want."

Chantley's eyes widened. Wasn't that a part of the lesson on karma? That she could choose her reaction to the situation. She knew this but, so far, had not applied it. It took this old lady to remind her of these morals. She reflected. *I'm no more vulnerable now than at any time over the past couple of years. I can continue with Sam or head off alone, but in either case, I must act out of courage.* She looked up and breathed deeply.

"Do you think I should get back with Sam?" she asked Lakeisha

"What's worrying you? Sam's good-looking, he's educated, he's nice. I guess you're looking for the perfect man. Take it from me; there's no such thing. If I were you, I'd grab him before another woman does."

Chantley nodded her head thoughtfully.

"I have something you can take," said Queen Josephine. She got up and picked a double-stranded chain adorned with a pendant from a shelf behind her. The round, enameled, sky-blue ornament, about an inch in diameter, featured a black snake curling around its outside perimeter, its head meeting its tail at the top. An anthropomorphic orange sun with bright eyes, a strong nose, and smiling lips lay emblazoned in the pendant's center, with stylized sunbeams emanating to the edges.

Chantley immediately liked it: she recognized the imagery. The snake represented rebirth, appropriate enough for a creature that disappears into the ground only to reappear later. The blue sky resembled the horizon, infinity, and the spiritual. The sun on the talisman glowed warm and bright, expressing courage, optimism and hope, and its slightly hemispheric, shield-like shape suggested protection. Chantley held it in her hands and instantly felt the doubt and insecurity of the past several days evaporate.

"How much is it?"

"Forty-five dollars." The old lady smiled ironically. "Even Mambos have bills to pay."

"Wow," exclaimed Lakeisha. "Go ahead and get it!"

Chantley took the gris-gris and, feeling her confidence rise with every second, slipped it around her neck.

Chapter Twenty-six

At eleven in the morning, Sam and Chantley exited the Interstate at Ocean Springs, Mississippi. After purchasing a few sandwiches, they pulled into a parking spot that hugged a beach along the Gulf Coast. They had left New Orleans a couple of hours earlier, quiet and awkward, each hesitant to start the conversation. Sam was driving, and Chantley, in the passenger seat, had her gaze trained on the scenery. The weather proved pleasant, and the highway picturesque as it wound through pine forests.

A wooden walkway, built several feet above the teal-blue ocean, led to an octagonal pavilion out in the water. The sea steamed in the sun and, on its swelling dark-blue breast, near the horizon, sailed several black ships entering or leaving Biloxi, rendered minuscule by the enormity of the bay. Chantley observed the scene, fascinated. The silvery rolling flatness of the Gulf, the pristine melding of the ocean with the distant horizon and the long-beaked pelicans diving head-first into the turquoise waters painted an exotic picture. The salty lushness and the powerful fishiness pervading the air contrasted sharply with the delicate and variegated grasses and blooms of the hills in India.

As they sat, their legs dangling over the pavilion's side, Chantley drifted into thought while Sam extricated his sandwich from its bag. She enjoyed her time with Lakeisha and felt grateful for her friendship, for drawing out her feelings and making her consider her situation deeply. In a way, she envied her friend. Lakeisha had everything together, and her life seemed to be progressing in a straightforward and uncomplicated manner.

"I've been out on the ocean before," Sam said, finally breaking the silence.

"Really?"

"Yes. In San Diego." His eyes twinkled. "Do you know that fish talk?"

"No."

"Yes. You go way out and see bubbles coming up in the most unexpected places."

"Really?'

"That's sharks singing."

"What?"

"That's whales wailing. That's tuna fish tuning."

"Tuna fish tuning?'

"Uh-huh. Clownfish clowning. Groupers growling. Everything howling, moaning, weeping and screeching."

Sam pushed his glasses up his nose. "And all these sounds gather together in the middle of the ocean and build up pressure until the waters can't stand it no more, and they push themselves up like hills coming from the deep, and the ships go sideways, and the sailors go sliding, and the passengers go puking."

She cocked her head and stared at him in askance. "Passengers go puking?"

"That's right. And that's just the beginning."

"Is that right?"

"Yeah. We didn't talk about swordfish swearing, lionfish lying, catfish cursing."

"Get out of here."

"It gets so bad that the sea can't take it no more. Fish drive the ocean crazy. It can't stand all that noise and bad language, and it beats the beaches, crashes the cliffs and batters the boats."

"What?"

Sam feigned seriousness. "Oh yes. Did you know most shipwrecks are caused by fish? Fish kill more people than anything. More than nuclear reactors, more than lightning strikes, more than volcanoes."

Chantley burst out laughing. "Are you quite finished yet?"

"The ocean," he concluded gravely, "is a noisy place."

The morning's uneasiness broke. Sam appeared to be the same humorous, inventive, incandescently intelligent Sam she loved. In an instant, she felt entirely at ease with him again. She smiled appreciatively.

Sam cleared his throat. "Chantley, why do we fight?"

The waves lapped softly against the wooden pilings. She pulled her hair behind. "I don't know."

"I like you a lot, and I guess you like me, but somehow, we get on each other's nerves once in a while. Is it because we're incompatible?"

"No," she quickly answered. Not any more incompatible than Vijay. "In fact, we hit it off immediately."

"That's true," said Sam. "I felt immediately attracted to you. It's a mystery to me why we get into arguments. I guess I must be more careful not to fly off the handle."

Everything would go well, then, suddenly, bubbles of discord would emerge. *What we argue about are not the obvious things; not money, words or specific action*s. Money issues are almost always about control. And that indicates inequality in a relationship. What happened in their past life? Did something unresolved erupt into the present?

"I am sorry about the argument," he said.

"Me too," she sighed. "And I shouldn't snap back or play the victim. Both of which, I guess, are connected."

Sam looked up. "How do you feel about me?"

She returned her gaze to the pelicans diving into the sea near the breakwaters. Her feelings for Sam, submerged for the last couple of days, returned with force. The episode in New Orleans had clarified many things, brought her confidence, and, more than that, revealed her deepening love for Sam. Their quarrel revealed as much. *Didn't I choose to stay with him?*

"I love you," she admitted. "At the same time, it's my life. I'm responsible for my situation."

He glanced at her, his eyebrows raised. "Wow! You're starting to adjust to your life here."

She fingered the pendant around her neck. "Let's just say that I'm regaining confidence." She waited for a moment. "How do you feel about me?"

"I love you. You're someone I can feel loyal to and take care of. For the first time, I've found someone to commit to."

Chantley felt the blood rising in her cheeks. "You never felt like this with anyone before?"

"In my family, most of the men left their women." He shrugged his shoulders. "I don't want to repeat the pattern." Sam reached into his pocket and pulled out a small black box. "I have something for you." In it sat a thin silver ring set with a heart-shaped red stone.

Chantley's heart pounded.

"It's a promise ring," he said.

"What's that?"

"It shows my commitment to you. In New Orleans, the truth hit me when I had to stay away from you for a couple of days. I want to be with you, always."

Chantley accepted the ring and admired it as the sun sparkled on the metal and the stone. "Which finger does go on?" she asked.

Sam rubbed his forehead. "I don't think there's any formality regarding that. You can choose any finger."

She slipped it on the ring finger of her left hand. *What exactly does a promise ring mean? Does this lead to an engagement or, maybe, marriage?* But Sam hadn't mentioned the future. When they started in Boulder just a while back, they were friends, maybe good friends, but the time spent together on the trip deepened her emotions until it made no sense not to admit it. She felt compelled to ask him about their future but wondered how to bring up the question.

Sam sat busily attacking his sandwich. She hesitated. Did she have the courage to bring up the issue? Was it acceptable for a woman to talk about these things? In India, serious matters were relegated to parents or other elders. *I'm not Indian anymore;* she reminded herself. *I'm American now.* She had to take charge. Yet, a cloud of nervousness descended on her.

"I really like DeAngelo and Lakeisha," she said, hoping he would take the hint.

"Uh-huh," he said, still engrossed in his lunch.

She tried again. "They're such a nice couple."

"That's right."

She decided to attack the issue head-on. "Sam, where are we headed?" she asked with utmost seriousness, gazing intently at him.

He looked up. "South Carolina, of course. Where else?"

Her earnestness, in light of Sam's cluelessness, descended into farce. She giggled. He shot her a puzzled look. "What's so funny?"

Chantley burst out laughing. "Nothing."

He shook his head. "Women are so complicated."

Chapter Twenty-seven

Chantley opened the car window, let the air blow through her hair, and smiled with satisfaction.

Sam admired her. "You're beaming."

The meeting with Queen Josephine filled her, after a long while, with self-assurance. "Let's say I'm a lot more secure. I'm starting to feel at home."

He nodded. "I'm starting to see different parts of you."

Just north of Mobile, on Interstate 65, they stopped to pick up a hitchhiker. He introduced himself with a soft southern drawl. "Hi, I'm Kent."

"Hop in," invited Sam.

Kent wore blue jeans, an army-surplus camouflage jacket, gray tee shirt, black sunglasses and army boots. His light brown hair, held in place by a red bandana across his forehead, reached his shoulders, and a beard's fuzzy beginnings sprouted on his face. He threw his backpack into the backseat, climbed in and shot a surprised glance at Chantley. She didn't mind the startled look. She had begun to expect it.

"Where are you going?" asked Sam.

"I'm heading to Montgomery."

"What's with the boots?" questioned Sam.

Kent laughed sheepishly. "I returned from a tour of duty in Iraq six months back. Since then, I've lived like a hermit in the mountains above Sedona in Arizona."

His voice was quiet and almost apologetic. Yet, despite his lean, youthful frame, Chantley sensed strength in him, both physically and internally.

"Being in Iraq changed a lot of things for me. I couldn't get back to civilian life right away. I needed the peace of the country and the time to get my head straight."

Chantley couldn't picture this soft-spoken, thoughtful man in a war zone. "What will you do?" she asked.

"I'm moving to an intentional community in Central Florida, but first, I'm visiting my parents to pick up my things."

"What happened in the war?" she questioned.

"The conflict in Iraq made no sense at first, but now I realize that our economic system makes wars inevitable."

She tilted her head at him.

"Our system depends on constant exploitation. It didn't start now; it's the culmination of hundreds of years of history.

Aboriginals and Third-Worlders bore colonization's brunt and fell into slavery, dispossession, and poverty, but now, it could happen to anyone, even in America."

Chantley understood his point. Didn't John and Lori, back in Taos, mention the same thing? At first, their battle was with classic colonization, with the attendant attacks on religion and culture, and later with American capitalism. Now, the battle shifted to globalization, colonization's secular and materialist descendant. But the roots remained the same.

"The system depends on cheap resources, low taxes and inexpensive, and back then, slave labor," said Kent. "It's unsustainable."

Sam glanced at Chantley. "What do you think? You must have studied this in India."

She remembered India as the world's first significant colony. "The East India Company, a British corporation, took possession of India. Not only did it conduct trade, but it also governed the country, collected taxes and even maintained its private army. And to protect the company's enormous profits, not to mention lucrative trade routes, the British Empire became drawn into conflicts around the world. It set the pattern for the present: constant warfare and an emerging supra-national elite with the rest, poorly paid, working for them."

Kent replied. "Many of the costs of this economic system—pollution, diminishing natural resources, the personal and sovereign debt—are untenable, and it's going to collapse. The past five hundred years were like an enormous Ponzi scheme, involving thousands of corporations and hundreds of countries."

"Like a post-dated check?" she questioned. "The illusion of having wealth now when nothing will be left in the bank in the end?"

Kent nodded his head.

"What do you think will happen in the future?" Sam asked Kent.

"It will fail, but not before it destroys most of us. It's completely unsustainable, and I see no other possible outcome. I think it's already started. These wars may be the tipping point."

Chantley understood. Karmically, the British Empire required so much violence to maintain itself that it couldn't last. So when the end came, it came quickly. "Is that why you're moving to an intentional community?"

"Yes. We have to gain sanity. I have to gain sanity," replied Kent. "Real wealth comes from the earth, whether it's minerals, water or agriculture. The rest is just shuffling money from one pocket to the other. I want to reconnect with the earth. I hope to find a sustainable way of living that doesn't entangle me in a system that will break apart."

"Isn't that just escapism? Don't you need to radically change the system instead?" asked Sam.

Chantley considered Sam's point. Mahatma Gandhi, one of the great critics of colonialism, wrote that economic power should remain in the hands of the smallest units of sustainable human organization: self-sufficient villages, which he believed to be the most equitable units of economy. He understood the innate violence of colonialism by the way it dealt with people and the land and concluded that such a system could not last. Unfortunately, after his passing away, Indian leaders believed his economics to be naive and retrograde and opted for massive industrialization instead. "Maybe you're right," interjected Chantley. "Halfway measures are not enough."

Sam stared at her. "I'm surprised you're agreeing with me!"

"Only in the fact that we need to make a full change. But a violent revolution is like a couple of dogs fighting. One day, one dog is on top, and the next, the other dog is on top. In the end, nothing changes."

Kent perked up. "The solution lies in the small, not the big. Small, self-sufficient communities all over the world. It is the opposite of globalization, isn't it?"

Sam cautioned Kent. "I admire your idealism, but I must warn you, in Colorado, many people tried to set up intentional communities, but most failed."

Kent nodded his head. "Yes, it's not easy. We've become so addicted to the kinds of things this economy brings that it's hard to change. We need to find a peaceful way of living. But it's not a group of hippies doing this anymore. Sustainable living is a movement, a revolt against globalization, spreading throughout the world. I want to try it. I have to try it."

*****

At Montgomery, they dropped Kent off and headed north to Atlanta on Interstate Eighty-five. They spent the next few hours chatting, unaware of the passage of time, while the landscape exchanged red clay for brown soil, pine for palms and low hills for flat land. Chantley relished Sam's company, appreciating the drive.

"You look real happy," observed Sam. "I should take a picture of you. You're glowing!"

She beamed. "I'm enjoying this trip," she said. "I found Kent's ideas interesting. They addressed the real issue: our relationship with the Earth." Yet, something felt missing. She rubbed her forehead. "I think the discussion of economics and culture is important, but in the end, the spiritual aspect of the Earth is most significant."

"What does 'spiritual' mean?"

"The essence of the spirit is sentience or consciousness. The Earth is greater than its material components."

"The Earth having personhood?" asked Sam. "You mentioned that before."

"Not a human person, but one nonetheless, connoting things like attachments and feelings, because at the heart of every exchange, whether personal or economic, lies a relationship. Relationships flow through persons."

"We do have an intimate relationship with our planet," admitted Sam.

"The first exploitation is that of the Earth; all other injustices flow from that. If we want to change how we treat each other, we must first change our relationship with the land."

"That's very perceptive," exclaimed Sam. "So, slavery and poverty are spiritual issues, not just economic ones?"

"Absolutely. There are karmic consequences in how we treat the land because it determines how we treat each other, economically, socially and individually."

"Does the earth bear karma?"

"Of course!" Chantley remembered one of her favorite stories from the ashram. "Once, overburdened by the karma of evil rulers, Bhumi Devi, Mother Earth's spiritual personality, took the form of a cow and approached Lord Vishnu for assistance."

"A cow?"

"What could be more appropriate than taking the form of a cow—an animal so forbearing, so gentle, yet as exploited as Earth herself?"

"Go on."

"Tears rolled down the cow's eyes as she related the devastation caused to her and the living entities she maintained. Vishnu, enraged to hear of the wickedness of the evildoers, descended in an Avatar form and destroyed the evil rulers and re-established righteousness."

Sam laughed. "Politicians meeting their match?"

"No other choice existed," explained Chantley. "According to the text, the Earth floats in the spiritual cosmos based on karmic balance—that good deeds counterbalance the bad. If negative karma is allowed to continue unchecked, the Earth will sink permanently into the netherworld—a place of terrible consequences."

"That's quite a story!"

Chantley shuddered to think of the present. How would it all end? In a bloody conflict, a violent settling of accounts? Or could America overcome its karma?

Gazing through the window, lost in thought, she yawned. They had an early start to the day, and tiredness set in. She leaned her head against the window. The engine hummed, and the wind flowed by ceaselessly.

She closed her eyes.

Chapter Twenty-eight

Upon arriving in Atlanta, they found themselves again stuck in rush hour traffic. "We've got to stop doing this!" she exclaimed. "We always arrive in cities at the wrong time."

"I never expected Atlanta to be so huge. This is like New York City!"

"Where shall we go?"

"There's a place I've always wanted to visit. It's called Stone Mountain."

"What's in Stone Mountain?"

"A park," replied Sam, "with a lot of history." They circled south of the city, drove past the airport and headed north on Route 285. When they arrived in the Stone Mountain neighborhood, the clock on the dashboard read five in the evening.

"I'm tired," remarked Chantley. "And it's too late to visit the park."

Sam agreed. "How about we check out another motel?"

"No," replied Chantley decisively, remembering their last attempt at a motel stay.

"So, where do you plan to spend the rest of the night?"

"You still have your tent in the trunk?"

Sam pushed his glasses up his nose and stared at her. "I thought you didn't want to camp in the country."

Chantley shook her head. "Don't worry; I've gotten over that."

Sam whistled. "What changed your mind?"

"I did. There's no use going through life without changing. I'm here in America. I have to accept that fact."

"That's smart," said Sam, nodding his head.

"I was just scared of letting go of everything I brought with me."

Half an hour later, they pulled into a campground. It contained a zone for recreational vehicles and a tent area set amidst the pines. A young blonde woman met them at the office. "You're looking to spend the night?" she asked cheerfully.

Sam glanced at Chantley, surprised at the friendly greeting. "Yes," he replied.

"Great," replied the manager. "We have washing machines, a common room and showers. For your convenience, there's also an outdoor cooking area with charcoal grills."

"We'll take it," Chantley exclaimed. Sam paid for the night.

"Sure," replied the lady, accepting the payment. "Enjoy your stay."

"Isn't this nice?" asked Chantley as they walked back to the car.

"It is, and I'm astonished at how she treated us. I guess Atlanta is the new South."

"Let's go to the grocery store," she said. "I want to cook dinner for both of us!"

Chapter Twenty-nine

On Sunday morning, the Fourth of July, Stone Mountain Park attracted a large crowd. Besides locals, visitors from across America, as well as foreign tourists, abounded. At the front entrance, a band played John Philip Sousa and evening fireworks were promised.

"I didn't expect this," said Sam, pointing to a group of Black families sitting on picnic benches as their kids played about, "given the history of this place." Japanese visitors clicked away with cameras at the mountain, advertised as the world's largest granite monolith, while hundreds of people waved American flags.

They began their exploration with the scenic train ride, which presented an overview of the park's features. Water sports at the lake's edge, a museum, a petting zoo in a barn, an auditorium seating several thousand, trails, picnic areas and a collection of old Georgia homes and antiques drew the crowds.

After returning from the train ride, they visited Historic Square, a collection of notable homes, repaired and transported from their original locations to present an idyllic vision of early life in Georgia. A couple of structures seemed nothing but huts; others were larger and more sophisticated. One magnificent antebellum home, replete with tall, white-washed wooden columns in its front and a formal garden in the back, dominated the square. Surrounded by lush lawns and pretty gardens, the place painted a picture of colonial domesticity, devoid of even a hint of social dysfunction.

But the presentation was too perfect, the paint too bright, the box curtain sets too precise, and the paintings of the ancient proprietors in stiff, formal poses too carefully arranged. The undeniable historical reality of slaves in these charming homes was conspicuous by their absence, carefully scrubbed out of existence. But the past could not be so easily erased. In the back of the mansion stood two slave cabins, a kitchen and a wash house—the domain of slaves, whose duties included cooking, cleaning and washing for their masters.

"There are a lot of ghosts here," she remarked.

"What do you mean?"

"Unsettled spirits who haven't found peace."

Sam imagined generations of African Americans walking the halls, working in the kitchen and toiling in the fields. This property carried their dreams, their struggles and their lives. His interest as a historian trumped his unease. "You're right, but real people lived in these houses. These places are how we remember them."

They walked back to the mountain and gazed at the three Confederate heroes—Robert E. Lee, Stonewall Jackson and Jefferson Davis—sculpted into the light-gray granite of Stone Mountain's vertical wall face. The enormity of the portrait certainly impressed onlookers. According to the park's brochure, the largest bas-relief carving in the world, and while the three men towered four hundred feet above the ground, the entire carved surface measured approximately seventy thousand square feet. A cable car, the size of a small bus, took them to the surprisingly flat mountain top, which stood a thousand-six-hundred-and-eighty feet above sea level. A thin lake curled halfway around the mountain's bottom, and in the distance to the west, he observed Atlanta's skyline. An unexpected wind swept across the top.

"Is this what you wanted to see?" asked Chantley.

Sam nodded his head. "I have mixed feelings about this place. The Ku Klux Klan had its rebirth here."

Chantley glanced at him quizzically.

"The KKK is an organization created in 1866, right after the Civil War, meant to roll back gains after slavery. At that time, it had a small following, engaging in assassinations, mostly of African Americans, but it died out in a few years. In 1915, a group of fifteen men, led by William Simmons, met at the bottom of this mountain and reconstituted the KKK, after which they climbed up here and burned a cross. They planned to reverse all advancements in civil rights by way of Jim Crow laws, murder, and terror."

"That's terrible. Are they still around?"

"After its re-establishment here, the KKK multiplied and spread racial hatred throughout America, especially in the Midwest. In the mid-1920s, fifteen percent of America's eligible population belonged to the Klan. This second incarnation died out in the 1940s after their leaders were exposed as murderers and rapists who engaged in political corruption. Nevertheless, there is a current version of the KKK, which has about five thousand members."

"How does that make you feel about being here?" she questioned.

Sam looked into the sky and thoughtfully rubbed his chin. "I've always associated Stone Mountain with the sufferings of Black Americans. But now that I'm here, I'm not feeling that at all."

"What are you feeling?"

"Hope. That it's possible for change to happen."

"That's quite a transformation! You always seemed so hopeless!"

"Something's changed," he said, winking at her.

Chantley laughed. Love can change people, bring hope, and round out the rough edges. Sam had also made a difference in her life, convincing her of her future in America.

He continued. "I think, maybe for the first time, that it's possible for all of us—black, white, Native American, and everyone else—to get along. Not just get along, but to live together peacefully."

"What changed?" she asked, knowing the answer.

"You. You've changed me. The longer I know you; the less important race has become."

Chantley shook her head, smiling. "I think you fell in love."

Sam nodded his head. "Loving you is more important than the color of my skin."

*****

After lunch, they cooled off at the water park with its slides, pools and fountains. They tried the Sky Hike—a trek through the treetops, visited the Great Barn, petted its irresistible farm animals, hiked a forest trail and watched boats navigating the lake.

As evening fell and the sky darkened, a crowd gathered on the spacious lawn in front of the mountain. Once boisterous, now only slightly hushed, they waited for the Fourth of July fireworks. Sam and Chantley retrieved a blanket from the car's trunk, stretched it out on the grass and lay next to each other. She stared as stars slowly materialized and reflected on the change in their lives. Did this park, this place, trigger the transformation?

Despite the history of racism associated with Stone Mountain, the present has trumped the past. She recalled Sam's statement: the fact that all races and peoples came here to spend an enjoyable day underlined the change. She looked at the now-illuminated carvings of the Confederate heroes and understood the appropriateness of their prominent presentation. The past could not be transcended by denial; only honesty could bring change.

She wondered what the three sculpted Confederates thought as they looked over the land they once ruled and the society whose dead bones this place so lovingly preserved. Do they rest in peace, and did their souls move on to contemplate other lessons? Or do they restlessly cling to a time and an empire that has undeniably passed them by? No, she thought, history has changed. The fact that she and Sam lay together on a blanket, in the middle of the South, celebrating a Yankee holiday, contained the surest sign of a more equitable future.

As nighttime arrived, the crowd waiting for the fireworks reached an astounding size. Thousands held multi-colored light-sticks in their hands, which, in the dark, rolled back and forth like waves racing across a cove.

By the time the show started and the mountain flooded with multicolored lights, Chantley, lying on her back next to Sam, felt exhausted but blissful. The day's exercise, while tiring the body, had mellowed her mind. She pushed her hair behind her ears. The day felt perfect.

She moved her right hand up, rubbed his chest, and grazed her cheek against his. Sam looked at her in surprise. She understood his reaction: so far, he had taken the initiative in their relationship. But a new confidence had taken root, and Chantley felt settled in her connection with Sam. Instead of needing to react to Sam's every action, she accepted an equal relationship. She reveled in the discovery. It felt easier and more enjoyable.

Sam pulled her closer, and they lay tight in each other's arms, oblivious to the world. As the first fireworks explosions started hesitantly and at a distance, she squeezed herself against him. Her toes tingled. She closed her eyes, and the gathering detonations, growing closer and louder and increasing in urgent frequency, rolled down from the heavens and crashed into her body. Shaken by their loud insistence, Chantley opened her eyes.

Instantly, the darkness dispersed as giant balls of red, white and blue exploded. She gasped. The thunder shook the top of her head, shivered down her arms, shot right through her gut, down her legs and throbbed through her toes, one after another, for many long minutes.

And as suddenly as a tiger disappearing into the dark, it ended. Chantley got up. Her chest and torso felt unexpectedly damp, and she shivered. Sam wrapped the blanket around them, and they walked back to the car, neither saying a word.

Chapter Thirty

The next day they stopped for lunch in Augusta, Georgia, at a restaurant enclosed by a white picket fence and bordered with red roses. Tables sat on a verdant lawn under live oaks whose branches trailed strands of Spanish moss. Waiters wearing pressed black pants and starched white jackets served them. Mint juleps abounded.

Chantley appreciated Sam's dressing up for the date. He sported a neat brown tweed jacket with a white linen shirt, a red-striped tie, dark-brown slacks and polished black shoes. She also dressed for the occasion in an ankle-length cream gown, a sleeveless white lace blouse and a thin indigo shawl thrown over her shoulders. She had her hair tied in a bun on top of her head and adorned it with blue flowers. She had decided, unusually, to put on a hint of makeup and noticed the days of travel in the southern sun had bronzed her skin, making her green eyes ever more striking. She noticed admiring glances from adjacent tables.

The restaurant, Sam's choice, revealed a whiff of romance. The Southern grace, manners, setting, high-backed chairs, crisp linen and silver place settings lent sophistication and naturally suggested a place for elegant lunches, dinners and receptions for newlyweds. She imagined brides in white strolling the lawns, their bridesmaids close behind holding bouquets of roses, with bridegrooms in black tuxedos being escorted to their tables.

Sam didn't have to go through the expense. She appreciated the small gestures—bringing her a bottle of water when she felt thirsty, covering her with a blanket when she fell asleep and holding the car door for her. But his generosity impressed her. The episode in New Orleans proved to be a clear turning point, and their relationship found solid footing.

She ate lightly, ordering only a salad with sides of cornbread and collard greens. She enjoyed the slightly bitter greens, a taste acquired from India, where *shuktas* were popular.

Sam put his fork down and looked at her. "When do you think a man and a woman should become intimate?"

Chantley's eyes rounded. *Is he talking about us?* "What do you mean?" she asked.

"You know, share a bed."

"Only after marriage," she blurted. Sam returned his attention to his plate. *Thank God he didn't push it. I appreciate his patience.*

She always felt that if she committed to a man, it would be full, with everything that came with it.

His question made her think. *How do I get Sam to take that next step? I'm ready to settle down. I've been entangled in desperate uncertainty for too many years.* Chantley would not bring up engagement or marriage; Sam needed to do that. After all, he did profess his love for her, and she for him. She reflected. In some ways, it was easier in India, a more traditional and conservative country. With an agreement reached, the path became clearly defined.

She stopped. I'm just dreaming. She looked around the gardens. I'm getting carried away by this place. Still, the romance of a wedding, the flowers, the rituals and the reception at a fancy restaurant wouldn't leave her. Would she wear a traditional red sari or a white gown? A Hindu wedding or a Christian one? She suddenly straightened with shock. Somehow, she hadn't considered this essential question. Her eyes widened, and she quickly shot a glance at Sam. What would he prefer? How would he feel?

"What?" he asked.

"Nothing."

"Come on," he insisted. "You looked terrified."

"It's nothing!"

"Seriously?"

"It's a girl thing," she answered, looking away. "I don't want to talk about it."

Sam scratched his head. "I have no idea what you're talking about."

Chapter Thirty-one

The next day, Chantley awoke feeling nauseous and bloated. The first couple of days were always more uncomfortable, and some monthly cycles felt worse than others. On these occasions, she preferred staying in bed until the cramps eased. But with Sam incredibly excited upon arriving in Charleston the previous night, she knew taking the day off was out of the question. She would have to manage.

She pulled herself out of her hotel bed and into the shower. She closed her eyes, letting the water flow down her body, the heat loosening her muscles and relieving the pain in her abdomen.

Sam knocked on the door. "Are you finished?'

"Almost." Noticing the steamed-over mirror, she realized she had lost track of time. She tied her hair with a towel, wrapped another around her torso and stepped out of the bathroom.

"Are you okay?" asked Sam, waiting beside the door. "You've been in there for a long time."

"Just some cramps."

"Oh, I see."

Sam showered quickly and escaped the bathroom, looking fresh and energetic. Chantley peeked at him. "Where do we go?"

"There's a place downtown called the Old Slave Mart Museum," he informed her after a couple of minutes of googling on his cell phone. "It's a logical place to start."

They checked out of the hotel and drove through town. Sam barely contained his excitement. He tapped his fingers nervously, whistled and sped along the road. The city, belying its divisive past, presented a genteel, laid-back feeling. The weather and scenery resembled Houston or New Orleans—subtropical and humid, with saw palmetto trees and magnolias at every turn. At nine in the morning, the temperature had already reached ninety degrees with matching humidity. The drive didn't last long, with the town being manageable in size, the roads broad, and the traffic, light.

In fifteen minutes, they reached the Old Slave Mart Museum, housed in a brick and stone building on a wonderfully picturesque, tree-shaded, cobblestoned street just a few blocks from Charleston Harbor. Soft breezes from the waters caressed Chantley's forehead as she stepped out of the car.

Sam held her hand tightly as they walked through the arched front entrance. To an uneducated eye, the structure would never divulge its original function as a slave market in the 1800s. A friendly guide at the museum greeted them. "There used to be dozens of slave auction houses in this area," he said. "Only this one remains, now converted into a museum. Just this part, where the auctions took place, is preserved. At one time, this property contained a kitchen for the slaves, a barracoon, that is, a slave jail, and even a slave morgue."

The introduction was fascinating. Forty percent of all slaves brought into America first landed in Charleston. Many of slavery's institutions—laws, politics, farming, banking and even slave insurance—took root in and bequeathed South Carolina with one of America's most racially divisive histories. The tradition implicated so many people—businessmen, politicians, police, farmers and financiers—that it, along with racism, stubbornly resisted reformation.

The museum contained a few relics from slavery, but more, it outlined the history of the Middle Passage and the role of Charleston as the center of the Interstate slave trade in America after the termination of African slave importation in 1803. More powerfully, the individual slaves' narratives lined its walls.

"There is so much history here!" exclaimed Sam. "Imagine the number of slaves who must have passed through here. What they must have felt; what they went through!" He read all the accounts and gazed reverentially at the displays. This must be sacred ground for him, Chantley imagined.

After wandering for about an hour, Sam walked to an elderly administrator sitting at a desk near the entrance.

"How may I help you?" asked the lady.

"I'm wondering about old plantations in this area," replied Sam hesitantly.

"What do you want to know about them?"

"I'm wondering how to find them. You know, if any are around."

"Of course," she replied. She pulled out a brochure and handed it to Sam. "Take this map: you'll find them here. Many are open to the public, and the entrance fees are quite reasonable. Charleston is home to many plantations."

Sam shook his head, smiling. Puzzled, the lady looked at him.

"I never expected someone to hand me a map of the plantations. That makes my search a lot easier."

*****

After consulting the brochure, they visited three of the best-known and most-visited plantations: Magnolia, Boone Hall, and McLeod, arranged in a rough semi-circle around Charleston Harbor.

As he drove, Sam filled Chantley in on some of the history and geography he had gleaned.

"Charleston was founded in 1670, honoring King Charles II of England. Located on an inlet of the Atlantic Ocean, it quickly became one of the continent's largest cities, trading in rice, indigo, deerskin, and slaves."

"Slaves?"

"That's right. During the Antebellum period, it grew into the only large American city with a majority-enslaved population. Charleston has an important place in American history. The first battle of the Civil War erupted at the close-by Fort Sumter."

She noticed the considerable number of steeples pointing up into the sky and the hospitable residents with genteel manners. "But people here are so friendly," she remarked, unable to reconcile the past with the present.

MacLeod plantation, closest to downtown, set on thirty-seven acres, with a colonnaded entrance at the end of an oak *allee*, contained a typical, white-painted antebellum mansion. To the side of the oaks sat rows of slave houses.

"Is this what you saw in your regression?" asked Chantley.

"A lot of the elements—the columns, the trees and the slave quarters to the side—are the same," replied Sam, "but this is not it."

The plantation offered interpretative tours, complete with expert guides. Chantley appreciated the depth of their knowledge and the sincere effort to present not only the history of the past owners but also the daily lives of the slaves and the traditions they brought with them from Africa. A unique subculture in low-land South Carolina called Gullah, or Geechee, grew from this experience.

"I like the way they don't gloss over history here," remarked Sam. Indeed, the place detailed the antebellum period, the Civil War era, and even the transition to freedom of its erstwhile residents. He wandered silently through the rooms, keenly observing everything, and in the slave quarters, rubbed his hands along the rough wooden walls.

Does he wonder if his ancestors lived in a place like this? How did they spend their days? How much did they suffer?

Magnolia Plantation presented another spectacular example of the plantation experience. Famous for its gardens, constructed in the English Romantic style, it drew visitors from around the world. Weddings and receptions set under the oaks seemed a common occurrence. The main hall, a combination of antebellum and seventeenth-century English royal country home, featured a colonnaded front entrance and a square tower with sloping eaves on its left corner. In addition, several single-room slave cabins constructed of wood and set on stone blocks a foot high kept the structures off the ground in case of regular floods. Each dwelling presented a specific aspect of slave history and culture. But this plantation, too, though familiar in some ways to Sam, did not spark any recollection.

They visited Boone Hall last. A superb example of plantation culture, it featured a stunning *allee* of three-hundred-year-old live oaks and a main house designed in the Georgian style. Here, guided tours and a live presentation of Gullah culture in the Theatre were also available. Eight original slave cabins, restored and containing life-sized figures, photos and historical relics, guided the visitors through the history of that period. But it, too, didn't match Sam's vision.

Their guide, a young green-eyed brunette with a sweet southern accent, filled in the details of plantation life.

"An interesting situation presented itself," she explained. "A working plantation resembled a small community, a village really, but while the races shared the same space, many rules existed, both spoken and unspoken, to keep them apart. Despite the house slaves' involvement with slave owners' families, in raising children, a very strict apartheid, a social stratification, kept everyone in their place. Despite everyday interactions, a deep uneasiness existed between the two groups. Slaves feared and obeyed the owners, while insecurity enveloped the slave owners. Outnumbered on their plantations, they lived in fear of rebellion. Stories of slaves killing their masters circulated constantly. In the mood of the times, white women, seen as being particularly helpless, were kept safely away from male slaves during resting times. Thus, male slaves had no access to certain parts of the main home, for example, where the families slept. And, of course, the slave owners carefully kept their weapons in a safe place."

Sam nodded his head. "If you replace the slave owner with the cop and the judge, it's obvious that the same roles are being played today."

First experiences set the stage for future interactions, just as childhood events determine adult behaviors, Chantley thought. Once the pattern is set, it persists, even if the original impulse disappears. As a result, it would take many generations to heal the consequences—the broken families, the violence, and the incarcerations.

*****

"What should we do?" asked Chantley upon returning to their hotel in the evening.

"We'll check out other places tomorrow," promised Sam. "Charleston is amazing."

She dropped to the bed, her legs shaking. "I'm drained."

Chapter Thirty-two

The baking late-afternoon sun only made Chantley's discomfort more pressing the next day. They had visited another two plantations without luck, and tiredness caught up with her. Not only did her body ache, but her mood changed. The exploration lost its appeal. She only wanted to return to the hotel and lie in bed.

"Let's go back," she said. "Who knows if the plantation you saw still exists? If it ever did."

"We still have time," countered Sam.

Chantley grimaced. *He's like a little kid off on an exploration.* She sighed. Might as well bear it out a bit longer.

They drove around the countryside to the west of Charleston. The land, a fertile patchwork of farms and forest, rolled out before them, and further west, gently rolling hills arose unassumingly from the ground. They drove past a couple of old houses, but neither proved interesting nor relevant.

Finally, at five-thirty, Chantley spoke up. "Let's get back to the hotel. I'm exhausted."

Sam peered up at the clouds and sighed. "Yeah, you're right." Chantley felt his disappointment: did the place they sought, even if it existed, survive the years? They drove silently down the double-lane road east toward the city.

Ten minutes later, Sam spied an old house, barely visible through a grove of beech trees, set in the middle of a hay field. He pulled over.

"How about that one?" he remarked. "Should we check it out?'

Chantley shook her head. "It doesn't look like any house we've seen so far. And it's sitting in a patch of tall grass."

"Last one today," assured Sam.

"It isn't very big; there are no slave dwellings, cookhouses or anything else," she protested.

"You're right," replied Sam. "But it won't hurt to check it out. This place raises my curiosity."

"You've been excited ever since we arrived in Charleston."

"Last one, I promise."

She didn't have the energy to resist. "Okay," she replied unenthusiastically, "let's go."

They disembarked and walked for about three hundred yards through the field. Fortunately, the just-cropped hay barely touched her ankles, and the sweet smell of cut grass clung to the ground.

They came to the line of beeches, tall and magnificent, each sporting several large branches and, beyond, discovered an area of overgrown grass, weeds and thorn bushes. Sam led the way, carefully pushing back the vegetation for Chantley. After twenty yards, they arrived at what used to be the building's back, now a gaping hole framed by broken and bent timbers and a large mound of earth upon which grew bushes and weeds. They walked to the front of the house and discovered a sizeable semi-circular porch. The once-white paint had faded into shades of brown. The front door, having disappeared, left a dark opening resembling a gaping mouth.

"The place is creepy," she remarked. While not as large or complete as the historical mansions visited, she quickly deciphered its past. The front porch, sprouting the remnants of two original columns, proved that the structure belonged to the antebellum period.

"It doesn't look like much," she said, comparing the place to the perfect homes they had visited.

"You're right," agreed Sam. "But remember, we're talking about a building that's possibly two hundred years old."

Sam looked at the brick walls and the large second-floor windows. "I get a sense about this place."

So did Chantley but what she felt was dread. A sense of melancholy and unease hung over the place. It could be her out-of-sorts mood, her tiredness, her pain, or maybe the sight of the wreck of this once-proud building, but something did not feel right, as if the old house held secrets it hesitated to reveal. And if it proved to be a slave plantation, the sufferings of its long-disappeared inhabitants would hang around like a dark cloud, discernible to sensitive souls.

Chantley swept bits of grass from her jeans and climbed up the porch, the steps having long disappeared. The boards creaked under her feet, and she circled holes in the wood. She followed Sam carefully into the building and stopped at the entrance for several seconds, allowing her eyes to adjust to the dark. Inside, years of dust covered the floors, generations of dried grass blew in and out of the rooms, while heaps of dead bushes gathered in the corners—a decades-long organic invasion destined to eventually overwhelm human order.

"Look at this!" he exclaimed, his voice rising in excitement. He pointed to a winding wooden staircase near the front door.

She stopped beside him. "But we've seen the same in other houses."

He rubbed his chin. "True, many antebellum houses have similar staircases, but this feels different."

Chantley couldn't share his excitement. Tired and slightly nauseous, she regarded the rickety steps warily. "I don't know if I trust them. They look rotten."

Indeed, the railing was gone, and the timbers, worn and broken, with yawning holes and missing planks, didn't feel worth the risk. South Carolina's humidity, not to mention ants, rats and termites, had done their job.

"I'll go ahead," he ventured. "You can follow me."

He gently stepped on the first stair, testing its solidity before climbing the next one. They came to a landing which, with its broken back wall, overlooked the backyard and the enormous mound of dirt. The sunlight slanting over the fields contrasted with the dark shadows of the house's interior, but the scene didn't lighten Chantley's mood. It felt oppressive. Sam walked gingerly across the landing and proceeded up the remaining stairs to the top.

They turned left, down the corridor and, several steps later, stopped at the entrance to a large room on their right. The doors had disappeared, and inside, bottles, rags, and rusty cans littered the floor while layers of graffiti colored the walls. Even while decaying, the house had sheltered indigents. The ceiling showed swirling, concentric rings of brown, like tea stains on a paper napkin, where rainwater had seeped through. Just a couple of dark wood panels still adorned the walls, hinting at the one-time richness of the place.

Chantley gathered in the scene. Despite the debris, the dust and the absence of furniture, this room, measuring over thirty feet long and about twenty deep, had been, literally, the master bedroom. It resembled many such rooms visited the day before. Large brown wooden beams lined the ceilings and across from them stood several windows that looked out over the mansion's front. The glass had vanished, as had the shutters. Sam walked over and peered out. Chantley joined him.

"Wow. This might be it," he said breathlessly.

"How so?"

He directed her attention to his fingers. "I know it proves nothing, but the way my fingers press against the window sills and the feel of the wood grain seems familiar."

"Are you sure? You're just caught up in the adventure."

Sam lifted his eyebrows and shrugged his shoulders.

She leaned out of the window. "I don't see the driveway you described in your regression. Nor any trees." The sun, low to the west, stung her eyes. "And no slave quarters."

Sam scratched his head. "You're right. But the trees could have been cut down, the slave quarters demolished, and the road swallowed up by the fields."

"We need something concrete, some real evidence."

When he looked back at her, she saw her comment had brought him back to earth. He rubbed his fingers again against the large-grained wooden sills. "I'm relying on my feelings. Many houses have windows overlooking their front entrances. Unless I come across something tangible, I can't be sure."

"How do we find out?"

"Let me retrace the steps from the regression," he suggested. He pointed outside. "I was looking straight ahead when I saw the commotion out front, just several hundred feet away."

"What did you do?"

"I immediately turned around and ran. When I came to the door, I saw the rifle hidden in an alcove." They walked away from the window and back to the door and, sure enough, noticed alcoves built into the walls on each side of the bedroom entrance, behind where the doors would have stood.

"What about this?" he asked.

She shook his head. "We've seen alcoves in the other antebellum homes."

"Let's keep going. I grabbed the rifle and ran down the stairs." They returned to the landing and proceeded down the rickety stairs. When they reached the columns on the front porch, Sam stopped. "I stopped here for a few seconds. Maybe I was bewildered by the whole thing."

"Why would you be taken aback?"

"I get the feeling that the whole thing came as a surprise to me. Maybe I was surprised that my fellow slave brothers and sisters revolted unexpectedly."

"Then what did you do?"

"I jumped off the porch and ran down the garden."

They hopped off the porch, and, in an exercise in imagination, Sam guided Chantley through the grass in a straight line from the house. "We're walking where the driveway would have led from the house to the front gate."

He pointed to the right. "The wall with the tall bushes to the side of the driveway would have been ten yards that way. Many slaves ran along its shadow to avoid being seen."

"How about you?"

"I ran down the middle of the road. To get to the gate faster, I imagine."

They walked through the pasture, and two hundred yards later, Sam stumbled upon a trough about five feet deep and three across. A natural barrier to farm equipment, it had been left unscathed and ran for a hundred yards in a straight line until the fold in the earth straightened out and disappeared into flatness.

"This would be the edge of the property," mentioned Sam, "where the driveway met the front road."

Reeds grew and dragonflies flitted in the dank, dark waters of the trench.

"Well, here we are," said Chantley, and sat at its edge.

Sam joined her and threw a clot of dirt into the water. The stale smell of decomposing vegetation emanated from the ditch.

"Yes," echoed Sam. "Here we are." A long pause followed. They looked at each other awkwardly.

Now what, she wondered. They had explored the property, and while it held promise and could be the place that appeared so vividly to Sam, nothing concrete tied them to it. Nothing they could hold in their hands; nothing that would shout out, 'this is it!' They had traveled across the country expecting something liberating, maybe even cathartic, that would change their lives and answer age-old questions.

She shook her head. *What questions? For what did we come looking?* The whole thing was anti-climactic. Chantley felt foolish. *How stupid! What would I find here?* She stared silently into the water for several minutes as the sky darkened. The lonely chirping of grasshoppers rustling in the fields exaggerated her sense of desolation. Her mood darkened.

"Even if this is the place, what does it prove?" she asked.

"Nothing."

She struggled to her feet. "Let's get going," she said, unable to bear it any longer.

"This is so disappointing and embarrassing," said Sam. "I feel like I wasted a whole month of my life. Let's get the hell out of here."

*****

As they got up, Chantley stubbed her right toe on something.

"What is it?" questioned Sam.

"Maybe a rock."

Sam peered down. "No, it looks like a bit of metal."

Chantley felt it with her fingers. "Yes, that's what it is." She turned around. "Let's go."

"Give me a minute. Let me check it out." The object, right at the water's edge, protruded less than an inch above the ground. Sam, using his fingers, dug around it. It proved to be larger and went deeper than I first imagined. As Sam pushed it back and forth, the water in the ditch swirled. A large part of the metal object lay submerged in it. After several minutes of struggle, it loosened. With a great heave, he pulled it up and laid it on the grass.

Wetting his hands with ditch water, he scraped the thick mud off the object. The metal knob, against which she had stubbed her toe, topped a four-foot long, one-inch-thick black metal column, rusted in several places. Two parallel metal rods, each a half-inch thick, two feet apart and bent into an arc, extended from the column. And the space between these two rods contained several black metal letters.

He sank to his knees. "I know exactly what it is!" he remarked.

"What?"

"Read the letters."

Chantley knotted her eyebrows. It read 'C,O,O,_,_, R,' and after a space, the letters 'R,I, V.' "I have no idea what this is."

"I do," said Sam in a hushed voice. "It's the name of the plantation. Cooper River."

Chantley examined it again. "I can see what looks like Cooper River, but I don't see the word 'Plantation.'"

Sam pointed to where the two curved rods ended. "Look. The thing broke off there. But I recognize the script, the shape—this hung over the front gates of the plantation. It's precisely what I saw in my regression." He grasped the object with his hands. "I can't believe it! I'm standing on the exact spot where those slaves got trapped at the gate and died."

"Wow!"

"And where I saw you back then," he added triumphantly.

The discovery stunned Chantley. They finally had tangible proof. Incredibly, it tied everything together.

"It's amazing," exclaimed Sam. "We met here so many years ago!" He jumped up, gathered her tightly, swept her off her feet and twirled her around.

Chantley screamed with pleasure and languished in his arms. He released her, and they sat next to the relic for many minutes, discussing its implications. For Sam, it solved the mystery of his ancestors and their relationship from previous lives. For her, it provided a bridge, not only between them but also with her connection to America. As they talked, the sun set, leaving just a patch of purple on the horizon.

But as they sat conversing, Chantley realized their conclusions had been too pat. The discovery proved to be just the beginning. The ghosts of the place argued in her ears. "Something doesn't seem right. My gut tells me that there's more to this story."

"Absolutely! So much more. The lives of the individuals who stayed here, their dreams, their hopes, their histories."

She shook her head. "I feel as if we are missing something."

"But isn't this exactly what I saw in Dr. Dyer's office?" His eyes shone with excitement.

She breathed deeply, as if recalling a faint smell in the air, sniffing a lingering doubt in the atmosphere. "I get a kind of restlessness about this place."

"What do you mean?'

"About us back then. I sense that we don't know everything. The reality is probably much more complex."

Sam shrugged his shoulders. "It's exactly as I described it during the regression."

"What happened after you met me here? Did you escape with the others?"

Sam shook his head. "No. I stopped here."

"Why wouldn't you escape the instant you had the chance?" she questioned.

"Simple. I was in love with you."

She rubbed her left temple. "Why did you run down the middle of the road instead of sticking to the shadows like the others?"

Sam shrugged his shoulders. "Maybe I was in a rush to escape."

"But you would have been an easy target. Isn't that why the others stuck to the safety of the hedge?"

Sam furrowed his eyebrows and scowled. "I don't understand all these questions."

Suddenly the truth struck her. She shivered. She hesitated for a second but realized that the question deserved, no, needed, to be asked. Her exhilaration vanished. A deep uneasiness descended with the darkening sky.

"Didn't you pick up a rifle in the bedroom before running down the stairs?" she asked in a quivering voice.

Sam looked blank. "So?"

"It makes no sense."

"Why?"

"A slave-owner leaving a rifle where a slave could pick it up? Don't you remember what the guide told us yesterday? That plantation owners always kept armaments away from slaves?"

Sam's eyes narrowed. He rubbed his forehead and started pacing. "What do you mean? Where are you going with this?"

"Many things don't make sense." She recapped her points. "You were in the master bedroom where a male slave wouldn't be at night-time. You had a rifle. The rebellion came as a surprise to you when it shouldn't have if you were a slave. You ran down the middle of the driveway. You stopped, recognizing me, at the gate. Finally, you didn't run away with the others." Chantley calmed her pounding heart. "Don't you see? It's so clear."

Sam shook his head in confusion. "What's so clear?"

Blood thundered in her veins. Yet she felt compelled to continue. "You must have been the slave owner, not a slave!"

Sam's face turned white. "That's ridiculous! Whoever heard of a black slave owner?"

He still didn't understand. She dreaded telling him, but it was the truth as far as she could see. She dropped her eyes. "Don't you see?" she whispered. "You weren't black. You were white. And you stopped instead of escaping because I was your wife."

Stunned, Sam remained silent for several seconds before bursting into a rage. "This is bullshit," he yelled. "You're making me out to be a white slave-owner?"

Chantley quivered. The truth attacked the very core of Sam's identity. "Sam," she pleaded, not daring to look at him. "What difference does it make now?"

"That's bullshit," he yelled again, infuriated.

"Sam, forget it. Think about the two of us. Can't we get on with our lives?"

He swore and kicked the ground. "This is the karma bullshit you've been telling me about?"

Chantley wiped the tears streaming down her face. "Sam, I love you."

"Leave me alone," he shouted, pushing her away. "I don't believe anything you say anymore. I'm getting out of here and away from you. I don't want to have anything to do with you."

Sam staggered away to his car. The nausea, cramps and unease of the past couple of days exploded in Chantley's gut. Overwhelmed, she fell to her knees in tears.

Chapter Thirty-three

Darkness covered the fields, and Chantley heard only the frogs croaking in the fields and her heart thumping in her chest. Panic enveloped her, and the stench from the ditch stung her nostrils. Repulsed, she blew it out of her lungs. She struggled up on shaking legs, swallowed hard, pushing nausea down, and stumbled across the hayfield. The quarter-moon's blue light illuminated the hushed landscape. Thorn-covered brambles cut into her ankles and her sandals stubbed against thick tufts of fescue.

After twenty minutes of groping across the ill-lit land, she arrived at the road where Sam had left the car. The road remained perfectly empty. Not a single house, automobile or even a streetlight could be seen. She gasped with fright and took a steadying breath. She was on her own. She stumbled over to the road's shoulder and discovered her suitcase, popped open, and her clothes lying strewn in the dry ditch next to the highway. Straining her eyes, Chantley fished around for her clothes, stuffed what she could back into the Samsonite, and snapped it shut. A few feet further, she found her shoulder bag. *Thank God Sam didn't drive off with my things.* She opened the zipper with shaking hands and checked inside. Her wallet and the tin box containing her address book were safe inside.

She sat the suitcase straight up on the side of the road and crumpled beside it. She angrily pounded the pavement with her fists. *No one ever treated me like this! What a horrible thing to do!* Tears of frustration came, softly at first, and when the gravity of her situation shrouded her in coldness, she wailed. *How did I end up with such a horrible man?*

Oh God, she whispered, *why did Sam drive off and leave me like this?* She had never felt so alone, so abandoned, lost in an unfamiliar countryside in the middle of the night. Please, God, get me out of here!

After a while, the panic lessened. She looked at the broken mansion sitting desolately in the middle of the field, its dark silhouette cutting into the sky. She shook her head. The moment she had approached it, something didn't feel right. Some secret unhappiness permeated the wooden bones of the place. What happened here?

Despite her despondency, she let her imagination take over. It was like she remembered something. She wore a pink gown, standing at the top of the now intact and shining stairs, her hair in curls, with old-fashioned red jewelry hanging on her ears and laying around her neck. The chandelier burned bright with candles. The house looked lively as slaves rushed about and guests wandered by. Step by step, she slowly descended, keeping her eyes down, navigating the stairway. At the bottom, the ladies greeted her, congratulating her on the preparations for the evening. She was the mistress of the evening. Near the front door stood her husband, tall and thin, with dark hair, wearing calf-high tan boots, tight pants and a black waistcoat, greeting the guests. Despite the dress of a different era and the change in race, undoubtedly, it was Sam. She hardly noticed his face. The relationship's feeling and mood remained the only proof she required.

He glanced at her and waved his hand, commanding her to join him at the entrance, where two visitors, a middle-aged man and his wife, their standing and wealth evident by their demeanor and dress, stood waiting. She walked over, offered a peck on the lady's cheek and offered the man a curtsy.

Chantley's husband smiled and glanced at her, yet she avoided his attention and gazed through the open door. Horses and carriages gathered in front of the house and lined the sides of the driveway. Her eyes followed the row of carriages and came to rest on one of the slave huts on the right side of the driveway. Warming their hands over small bonfires, slave men sat outside their cabins.

She examined them, one by one, searching for someone in particular.

Her husband brusquely tapped her right shoulder. Startled, she looked at him. He shot her an angry look and slammed the door shut.

A sudden gust whistled across the fields, breaking the spell. Chantley shivered. The wailing wind returned her to dark reality, and the same feeling of unhappiness descended upon her. Despite the wealth the place displayed in her imagination, a deep dissatisfaction lay beneath. She pursed her lips. Sam had been displeased with her in their previous life and now, in this life. *What caused it? How can I explain it?*

Sam, she asked, *why are you angry with me?* She examined her heart: besides the hurt and anger, she felt regret. Regret that it had come to this, that she had fallen in love and been rejected again. The same issue arose: he couldn't accept her without acknowledging what she believed.

Self-pity overwhelmed her. *Why are all these things happening to me? Am I being singled out for some special punishment?* She thought of her mother. Her eyes widened, and she sat up suddenly. In her infatuation with Sam, she had forgotten about her mother over the past few weeks. The anxiety present at the beginning of her American sojourn returned in full force. *Mom, I'm sorry I forgot about you. I've been so stupid; I deserve this.*

A car's high-beams, maybe a mile away, punctured the night. Chantley hurriedly wiped the tears off her face and straightened her hair. Finally! Someone! She followed the car's lights slowly navigating the darkness, turning around curves, disappearing behind hayricks, glimmering between trees, and reappearing on the road. As it approached, however, fear took over. Who would be out in the middle of the night? Her legs wobbled. *Should I run?* A cold panic shook her. She decided to drop everything and dash back to the house. But her legs froze. She couldn't move.

Before she knew it, the slow-moving car rolled up and, with screeching brakes, stopped beside her. A window rolled down.

"Good Lord, what you doin' there?" It was a man's low strong voice.

A light inside the vehicle turned on, and Chantley saw an old black man with gray hair and a slight build sitting in the driver's seat. Dressed in a black suit, he had a clerical collar around his neck.

"Who are you? And what you doin' in front of that ole haunted house?"

Chantley relaxed slightly and started breathing again. The man's demeanor felt not at all threatening. She opened her mouth, but no words escaped.

"Well, are you goin' stay here all night?"

"No, no," she blurted. *He might leave without me!* "Please. I need a ride into town."

"How the heck did you end up here in the middle of nowhere? If it weren't for givin' a sermon at the church in the next town, I wouldn't even be in the county."

She blankly nodded her head.

"Well, you need a ride or not?"

Chantley rushed over, opened the passenger door, threw her things inside and jumped in.

"Thank you," she said, her voice trembling. "Thank you so much."

Chapter Thirty-four

In the fading twilight, Chantley checked the address. The black metal numbers on the brown wooden door of this unassuming bungalow matched the one in her notebook: 4330 Olive Street in Silver Springs, Maryland, a suburb of Washington, DC. She hesitated momentarily, then pushed the button.

Mrs. Moorthy, a slender elderly Indian lady, wearing wire-rimmed glasses, with gray hair reaching her shoulders, opened the door. A moment of silence ensued, followed by the shock of recognition. "Chantley, my dear, is that you?"

Chantley broke into a smile for the first time in two days. "Yes!"

Mrs. Moorthy rushed forward and planted a kiss on her cheek. "My," she exclaimed. "You have changed so much! The last time we saw you, you were just sixteen! Anand," she shouted, glancing back, "come here and see."

An old Indian man with medium-brown skin, a mostly bald head and wearing glasses, walked over. He looked thin, an old man's thinness, with a lean frame, sagging skin and a slight pot belly over which sat a belt holding up his trousers.

"I'm so happy to see you!" exclaimed Chantley. She rushed over and hugged him.

"Chantley! What a happy surprise!"

Mrs. and Mr. Moorthy looked precisely as she remembered them when they left the ashram five years ago to join their son in America. Chantley and the other ashramites had followed them to Mysuru to see them off at the airport. The elderly couple had promised to return regularly. Still, Chantley understood, as did the others, that with Guru-ji's departure, the pull of family superseded the ties binding them to the ashram.

Mrs. Moorthy examined Chantley's face. "You look exhausted."

Chantley blinked rapidly as her eyes moistened, sadly recollecting the struggles of the past two days. By the time the old preacher had dropped her off in Charleston, it had been almost midnight. After moping in tears, confusion and pain the next day, she bought a bus ticket to Washington and made her way to her old friends.

The Moorthys needed no explanation, nor did they ask questions. They were, in a sense, family: Guru-ji's extended family. Based on their seniority and maturity, they had, over the years, become surrogate parents to many of the young ashramites. Loved by all, they, in return, loved all.

Mrs. Moorthy grabbed Chantley's hands and pulled her in. "Come, eat something," she ordered. Hungry, exhausted and feeling at home after a long while; the words poured like nectar on Chantley's ears.

*****

After dinner, Mrs. Moorthy cleared the dishes from the circular four-seat wooden table located in a recess next to the kitchen while Chantley wiped the tablecloth clean.

"Sit down, Chantley," said the old lady. "I need to show you something." Surprised, with eyebrows raised, Chantley looked questioningly at her. Mrs. Moorthy retrieved a file from a two-drawer wooden filing cabinet that supported the living room television. She returned and sat on a chair, clutching the file.

"What is it?" questioned Chantley, bewildered.

Mrs. Moorthy retrieved a sheet of paper and handed it to her. "Please read this," she said. Wide-eyed, Chantley took the document.

Dear Moorthy-garu,

I hope you are doing well. Please forgive me for not connecting with you since you moved to America. I hope yours and Mrs. Moorthy's health are well. My respects to your son.

We are all doing well at the ashram, though, with Guru-ji's passing away, we are feeling lost and somewhat directionless. The students still come, and although we are quite busy, we don't feel the same energy. I'm sure you understand.

Chantley is doing well. Growing up at the ashram is a wonderful blessing for her; the love and support that you, your wife and the others provided have helped me raise her and, in many ways, compensated for her mother's absence. She has turned out to be the most sensitive, intelligent girl imaginable. I am so proud of her.

She is, at heart, still a young, sweet girl, but she is becoming an adult in front of my eyes. With each passing day, it is also clear that, as she grows up, the ashram will not be able to provide what she needs. She will, I know, eventually seek her future outside. I see signs of this already. She seems to be looking for something. She is a young woman and will soon seek her life's companion.

Julia left us when Chantley was just three years old. And despite her mother's absence all these years, Chantley has never forgotten her. As her eyes open and she spreads her wings, the questions regarding her mother will become important. You see, I worry about her future.

I am writing to ask you for a small favor—one I hope will not take too much of your time but is vital to me. Actually, for my daughter. I have been unable to correspond with Julia for many years; perhaps she has moved away from Boulder. However, she does have relatives in Pittsburgh, which I understand, is not so far from Baltimore. If you could find out what happened to Julia, I would be most grateful.

If she can be located, Chantley would be able to reconnect with her. If not, my daughter can find closure and move ahead with her life. Despite my doubts and fears, I do need to find out. When the time comes, when these questions naturally enter Chantley's mind, I want to be able to share the answers with her. I thank you in advance for all your help.

Dear Moorthy-garu, we all miss you and hope that you will be able to visit us.

Yours in the service of our beloved Guru-ji,
Michael Armstrong

"We received this letter two years after moving here," explained Mrs. Moorthy. "And your father passed away three months later, before we could reply."

"You expected me to come!" said Chantley.

Mrs. Moorthy nodded her head. She pulled out another piece of paper from her file. She gazed sadly at Chantley. "I'm sorry, my dear," she said. "When I got this, I didn't know whether to send it to you."

Chantley grabbed the correspondence, an official one bearing a government seal filled with incomprehensible jargon. Her mind went blank. She dropped the letter onto her lap with shaking fingers.

"What is this?" she questioned.

Mrs. Moorthy removed her glasses and sighed. "Your mother died in a car crash years ago. This is the certificate we obtained from the government."

"My mother died?"

"Alcohol was involved," whispered Mrs. Moorthy. "Your mother was an extraordinarily sensitive woman. I always felt that she could never be happy. She kept looking for something in her life. She couldn't find it at the ashram. She didn't find it in her marriage. Maybe she searched for it in the bottle."

At that moment, Chantley aged ten years. She indeed was an orphan with absolutely no one in the world. Utterly, totally, alone with every childish pretense stripped cruelly away. Tears choked her. Her sheltered upbringing didn't protect her, couldn't shield her, from the realities of a cold, frightening world. Didn't Sam warn her of this? That she wasn't prepared for what the world would throw at her? Sam, despite his thoughtless delivery, had been right. 'Who gives birth to a child in a foreign country and leaves her there?' It hurt when he said it, but he was right.

She revisited her father's letter. He had been spot-on in so many ways. Didn't he state his doubts, his suspicion and his fears? He must have surely felt in his heart that her mother was gone. And that Chantley would search for her. If only he had been alive to reveal everything!

The fog of illusion lifted. Chantley examined her heart. Deep down, she also known her mother had left this world. Yet, unwilling to accept it, she had transplanted that sobering reality with the beautiful vision of running across a park on a warm sunny day into the arms of her loving mother under a sheltering tree. Maybe she adopted this warm fuzzy fantasy precisely because she didn't want to accept a truth that should have been obvious all these years.

She shook her head. She had suffered two terrible shocks in the space of two days—first Sam and now her mother. Everything gone. Her entire American experience collapsed into confusion.

Eventually, the sadness and pain dissipated, and numbness took over. Stunned, she sat staring blankly into space.

"You need to lie down," whispered Mrs. Moorthy. "Let me help you down to your room."

Chantley woke the next day with a dull, distant headache that felt somewhat comforting. The pain, to a degree, blocked her thoughts. She spent the daylight hours in her basement room, wandering between emptiness and intermittent pondering of her future, feeling dizzy and cold, floating like an ethereal spirit, disconnected from herself.

In the early evening, Mrs. Moorthy insisted on Chantley eating dinner. Chantley came upstairs but swallowed the food half-heartedly.

"Let's look at my photo album," said the old lady after dinner. "Maybe that will cheer you up."

The two women retired to the living room, sparsely populated by a khaki-colored sofa, a glass coffee table with wooden legs, the filing cabinet and the television. Pictures of the Moorthy's son, Guru-ji and the ashram hung on the walls.

Mrs. Moorthy brought out her photo album and sat beside Chantley on the sofa, reminiscing. The first photo, sepia-tinted, showed the Moorthys as a young married couple at about the time they left their comfortable home in Bangalore, a couple of hundred kilometers northeast of Mysuru, to help Guru-ji establish his ashram. Next, Mrs. Moorthy pointed to a series of faded old pictures showing the ashram's early days before it started attracting Westerners, consisting of a small cluster of simple buildings constructed with indigenous materials and occupied by local people.

A few pages further on revealed growth. The number of buildings increased, the ashram looked more settled, and a relatively smooth dirt road replaced the rocky path to the top of the hill. Chantley's parents moved in at this time, harbingers of yoga aficionados to come in future years. The ashram changed as Guru-ji's popularity grew, and his Western tours became more successful. Housing for visiting students appeared, constructed of more sophisticated materials, indoor toilets, and a large meditation and yoga hall. At the same time, the state replaced the dirt road with a paved one.

The growth attracted not only visitors but also afforded employment to the locals. The photographs became crowded as gardeners, cooks and guides, what to speak of yoga teachers and Ayurveda instructors, found work there. Mrs. Moorthy turned the page, and suddenly a picture of Vijay stared back. Chantley recoiled.

"What's the matter, dear?" questioned Mrs. Moorthy.

Immediately, the void and numbness dissolved, replaced by heart-wrenching sadness. Chantley couldn't help comparing him with Sam. With Vijay, everything went well until the disastrous end. She thought they had climbed the mountain with Sam until she fell right from the top. *Which one was harder? Who did I care for more?*

"We were in love."

Mrs. Moorthy wrinkled her forehead. "I never knew that."

"It happened after my father died, just last year. Vijay was the first man to show interest in me." She shrugged her shoulders. "And maybe I was naïve."

The old lady comforted her. "What happened, happened for a reason."

Chantley sighed. "I don't know if I'm ever meant to have love in my life."

"There will be others."

Chantley shook her head. "I just broke up with someone else." She related the story of her relationship with Sam, the exploration of their karmic past, their travels and challenges. "I'm terribly confused and lost," she confessed.

"Why?'

"Sam and I were sure we shared a love from our past lives."

"What makes you think you didn't?'

"You mean we did?"

"Maybe. Guru-ji said that love is remembrance, either in this life or from a previous one."

"If it's remembrance, how do we know if the memory is good or bad?'

"Many times, you don't. Sometimes, strong emotions, good or bad, from past lives are confused with love. This especially happens in instances of love at first sight."

Chantley nodded her head. The explanation made sense.

"Even though the soul remains eternal and pure, it carries karmic reactions, like 'airs' or 'scents,' from one body to another."

"You're saying my relationship with Sam had some negative karmas attached to it?"

"I think so. From everything you've told me, it's clear that some discord, some unfinished business, remains from when you were husband and wife in your previous lives. For example, you mention that he doesn't consider your point of view or respect your feelings. That's why the house in South Carolina felt like an unhappy place. It's clear that even married, even in love, you shared some unresolved unhappiness."

"Isn't it strange, in fact bitterly ironic, that Sam, in this life, sees himself so strongly as a black man?"

"Yes, and no. What creates karma is identifying ourselves in material terms, such as race, religion, ethnicity, gender and so on."

"What do you mean?"

"I may identify myself as a female right now, but in the next life, I might end up as male, white, black, and so on. These are the dualities of life. These things change. But the soul, our real identity, is not male, female, black, white, Native American, Christian, Muslim or Buddhist. It transcends these dualities."

"Isn't it a cruel joke for a black man to have been white in a previous life?"

Mrs. Moorthy pondered the question. "Do you know what the basis of all morality is?"

Chantley rubbed her forehead. "The golden rule?"

"Yes. Do unto others as you would have done to you. You can't understand another person until you stand in their shoes."

"Okay." Chantley was puzzled over the turn the conversation was taking.

"I'm saying that the golden rule is not just a rule but reality. We really do appear in other people's skins. It's the only way we can experience what other people go through. If we didn't end up in other people's skins, the golden rule would have no meaning. It connects us all. Reincarnation makes the golden rule real."

"So, this isn't a question of race but a spiritual issue?"

"Absolutely." Mrs. Moorthy pointed with her finger as if tracing a painting on the wall. "Sam may have been a white man in a previous life. And before that, a Native American. Or Chinese or East Indian. But thinking of ourselves as white or black, rich or poor, male or female, this misidentification only causes pain. To learn certain lessons, souls take on different bodies for different karmic reasons."

Chantley pictured Sam in her mind. Her anger was gone. It must have been impossible for him even to entertain the idea that he might have been other than black in a previous incarnation. Being black—racially and culturally—was very important to him. Her concepts of karma, and her cultural constructs, collided with his self-perception and created an intolerable state of affairs. She understood his dilemma. He couldn't accept her without accepting her ideas, despite loving her deeply. "How does Sam overcome this?"

"Karma is the teacher. He will learn."

"What should I do? Is this a dead end? Will I ever be loved?"

"Don't worry. If the love is real, it will manifest itself." Mrs. Moorthy reached out and held her left arm. "You have to accept what happens. You have no choice."

Chantley's gloom and restlessness disappeared. Mrs. Moorthy's explanations satisfied her and helped her see where she and Sam went wrong. Her past with Sam became clearer. After all, they had acted according to karmic patterns long pre-determined. With understanding came peace.

Chantley took a deep breath. She had learned one thing at least over the past couple of months. She needed to approach whatever life threw at her without fear and fully embrace its potentialities.

She nodded her head. It was the only way left for her to survive and, maybe, even to thrive.

Still, one question remained. "What is the point of all this? I understand that as we progress from one body to another, we learn and grow, but will we continue this process forever?"

Mrs. Moorthy smiled. "The point of karma is to get out of karma."

"How do we do that?"

"We are spirit souls on a journey through this material life. At a certain point, having reincarnated enough times, we realize that our real identity is eternal, that we are eternal souls, beyond all material designations and thus perfectly equal." Mrs. Moorthy closed the photo album. "When this happens, another step appears."

Chantley eyed the old woman expectantly.

"Don't you remember Guru-ji telling us that spiritual love destroys karmic reactions?"

"Spiritual love? What's that?"

"Guru-ji described it as love for the Divine. If you pour water on a tree's roots, it nourishes the entire tree. Spiritual love is like that."

Chantley shook her head, wide-eyed. "I don't know if I'm ready for that!"

"Don't worry." Mrs. Moorthy laughed. "That's a rare attainment. For now, concentrate on your karma."

"My karma?" questioned Chantley. All this time, they had been discussing Sam. "What do I need to learn?"

Mrs. Moorthy smiled. "You'll see."

Chapter Thirty-five

Sam sat on the edge of his bed in a cheap motel room with the lights off. South Baltimore's industrial area, broken-down, tired and defeated, provided an apt metaphor for his mood. Cars whizzed by on the overpass next to the motel, trucks rumbled on the road below, tugboat sirens echoed from the bay, and, in the distance, near the harbor, boxcars clanged along railroad tracks. He had reached the bottom, life was defeating him, and he wasn't sure he cared anymore. He had no career, money, or future, and the woman he felt closest to in his life couldn't be further away. The last time he felt this hopeless was when he ended up in jail years ago.

Instinctively, he pulled out his cell phone. He hesitated. Would Ma pick up the phone? He felt too fragile to deal with Grandma. He dialed the number and waited.

"Sam, where are you?" Ma answered his call.

He winced. He hadn't informed his family of his travels. "In Baltimore."

"Baltimore!" she exclaimed. "What are you doing there?"

"I came looking for the plantation our family came from."

"Really? Did you find it?"

"We saw a place that might have been. But I don't know."

"What happened to your friend?"

"We got into an argument."

"Is she with you?"

"No, I left her in South Carolina." His voice suggested the finality of their break-up.

"You sound as if you left her by the side of the road."

"That's basically what I did."

"Oh Lord!" exclaimed his mother. "That's awful. Why did you do that?"

Sam couldn't answer. Ma was his moral compass. Her disappointment echoed in his heart.

"Sam, you can't get angry at people like that. Whatever it is, you need to forgive people for their wrongdoings."

He couldn't contradict her.

"You go apologize to that girl. I never raised you like that. We aren't that kind of people."

Her advice, as usual, was right. But he couldn't do it. "I can't see her again," he mumbled. It would be too painful.

"Grandma wants to talk with you." Before Sam could object, his grandmother was on the phone.

"Your Ma says you broke up with that white girl."

Sam held the phone against his forehead. He didn't need a confrontation.

"Maybe that's a good thing," she continued.

"What do you mean?"

"What's the point of running around the country with that girl? It's not what you need to do."

Unsurprisingly, she was giving him a hard time. "I'm tired," he said. "I don't need a lecture right now."

She ignored him. "Tell me what's going on."

Wearily, he complied with her demand. "I thought if I learned where I came from, I would know what to do in the future."

"Something happened." She was too cagey not to pick up on the context of his conversation. "What is it?"

"We came to South Carolina to visit some plantations..."

"Yes," she interrupted. "You've always been talking about slave days. What did you find?"

"Not what I expected," he mumbled.

"Uh-huh. I knew this would happen."

"What do you mean?"

"You've always going around with your head in the clouds. If you could be a bit more practical, you'd be successful. You're just wasting your life."

"It's not like that," he argued.

"Get your act together!" she demanded.

She wore him out. "Talking to you just gets me so frustrated." He hung up the phone. Exasperation overwhelmed him, and he gave in to the tears that had threatened him all day.

Why didn't it work out with Chantley? A lot was plain miscommunication—due to cultural differences—maybe not. DeAngelo said he was too intellectual and didn't give space to his emotions. One thing was true—he didn't have experience in equal relationships with women, and when he found real love, he didn't know how to deal with it.

I'm not a bad person. It isn't entirely my fault. Chantley's sensitivity clouded everything. He scratched his head. Something inexplicable kept coming between them. She is right about karma: these issues come from a previous life.

He shook his head. There was no use hiding the real reason: the devastating collision between his relationship with Chantley and his self-identity. The episode at the plantation rolled in his mind like a strange dream. He had imagined that discovering the past would be the key to his future, but his search for identity had, at a profound level, collapsed. His eyebrows furrowed. He'd always been of two minds about America; now everything seemed hopeless. *Life here is unbearable. Should I pick up and leave? Go to Africa? Would the answer be there?*

He got up and glanced out the window. Across the road, a lone streetlight burned against the darkness. *Was he a white man in his previous life?* He rolled the question around in his mind. At one level, he knew race to be a malleable concept. He had white genes, while many white people had black ones. But in America, the cultural aspects of race and not the genetics mattered more.

He understood his dilemma: Could he accept a subordinate role, the status quo that this country assigned to African Americans? Sam shook his head. Or could he go through life paying no attention to the color of his skin, as if the differences didn't exist? That was impossible.

He tapped his fingers against the window and remembered Frantz Fanon. What did Fanon have to say about this state of affairs? Fanon described it as a neurotic situation. He wrote about rising above racism, above this absurd drama, and rejecting the two terms as equally unacceptable. The goal was to, through himself, reach out to the universal.

Is that the answer? Why should I allow myself to be stuck in what the past determined? Fanon had written about not becoming enslaved by the institution of slavery and rising above its inhumanity.

Sam jumped up and pounded his right fist into his left one. A revelation overwhelmed him. *Exactly! I came to South Carolina not to re-experience slavery but to transcend it! That's what this trip is all about!* Besides, he didn't want to become bitter like Grandma, angry with the hand he had been dealt. He would much rather be forgiving, like Ma.

The answer to his dilemma became apparent. Sam needed to start over. He took stock. With a degree from a good school and the necessary intelligence to change things, he was more qualified than many people. He didn't mind working hard. *I can find a job or start a business or go into teaching. By taking care of myself, I can take care of others.* Taking responsibility is the right thing to do.

For the first time, he heard children playing on a basketball court behind the motel. He opened the window, breathed deeply, and felt liberated. Tomorrow, he would start the next step in his life. *But I have one thing left to do.*

Chapter Thirty-six

As Chantley sat eating breakfast the following day, her cell phone rang. She bolted upright. Was it Sam? Who else had her number?

"Yes. Hello?"

"Chantley?" It was Sam. It stunned her that he would call again. When he left, it felt final.

"Yes?"

"I'm wondering if we can meet. I need to talk to you."

She examined her feelings. The conversation with Mrs. Moorthy had changed things. Her anger had dissipated. Yet, Chantley hesitated. Did it make sense to reconnect if he didn't understand the nature of the relationship in their past lives? The single truth of their relationship was that they approached life from two different places.

Sam interrupted her thoughts. "I'm not asking for anything. I only want to share an important realization with you."

"Where are you?" she asked.

"In Baltimore," he replied. "And you?"

"Near Washington, D.C."

"Can I come over and meet you?"

Mrs. Moorthy leaned over. "Is that Sam?"

Chantley nodded her head. "Hold on," she told Sam. She muted the cell phone and turned her attention to the old lady. "He wants to meet me. Do you think I should go?"

"It's up to you."

Chantley rubbed her forehead. *Okay, let's see what he says, even if it's just goodbye.* Closure is better than regret. However, meeting him at the Moorthy's would be uncomfortable. She preferred a neutral place. "Is there a park or coffee shop where we can meet?"

"Hold on, let me check." After a minute, he answered, "There's a park near Annapolis called Quiet Waters Park."

"Where's that?"

"It's a half-hour from you. I can pick you up."

*****

Mrs. Moorthy opened the door. Chantley examined Sam. He dressed in the same clothes he'd worn in Boulder when she first

298

met him, right down to the hat. She tensed, and her cheeks stiffened.

A flash of concern crossed Mrs. Moorthy's face. "Are you going to be okay?"

"I think so," answered Chantley.

"Fine. Don't be long, and call if you need anything."

"Absolutely."

Chantley picked up her shoulder bag and walked to the car. Thirty minutes later, they arrived at the parking lot at Quiet Waters Park, which bordered South River on Chesapeake Bay.

They followed a trail into the trees, taking a path along the river, walking past jetties and boats. The area proved to be luxuriant, green, and populated with large trees. Finally, they came upon an empty octagonal pavilion constructed of brown wood and sheltered by a roof, near the water. Chantley sat on one of the chairs in the structure and placed her bag on an adjoining one. Sam pulled up a chair next to her.

He avoided looking at her. "I feel humbled," he started. "In a way, I've never been humbled before."

"I had to hitch my way back to Charleston in the middle of the night," she said, gazing at the water. The words came matter-of-factly. "Then I dragged my things to the bus station in Charleston and came to Washington to my friend's place."

Sam cleared his throat. "I want to apologize. About leaving you like that." An awkward silence ensued, leaving both staring into the distance. "I used to see things in black and white." He managed a nervous smile. "But life can be shades of gray, and sometimes, black can be white and white, black."

While showing greater understanding, his apology did nothing to relieve the distance created by the past few days' events. Chantley tapped her fingers awkwardly on the chair. "What do you want to talk about?" she asked, cutting to the chase.

He dropped his eyes. "The whole thing blindsided me," he mumbled. "I don't want that to be the last thing you remember about me. I'm not like that. Let's part on good terms if we don't see each other again." Sam's voice showed no trace of anger or recrimination. She relaxed and let her defenses down but couldn't find any words to share with him.

The silence stretched for several minutes. The days spent together blew through her mind like a dream. And felt as transient as one. She appreciated Sam reaching out to her, but the dialogue only emphasized the disconnect. What else could be said? Despite the warm weather, her fingers felt cold. The time had come to end things.

"Thank you for coming to see me," she said. "I appreciate it." She got up, straightened her hair and reached for her shoulder bag.

It slipped from her grip and fell to the floor. The tin box dropped out, and the cover popped off, scattering the contents.

Sam jumped off and snatched the pieces of paper threatening to fly away. A photograph scampered across the pavilion's wooden floor, and he grabbed it before it fluttered away. As soon as he saw it, his expression changed.

"Who is this?"

Chantley glanced at the photo and turned white.

"It's someone I knew," she mumbled. "Someone from India."

Sam rubbed his chin. "How long ago was that?'

"Last time I saw him was a year ago."

"And you still have his photo?"

She trembled. "He means nothing to me now."

Sam placed the photograph in front of her. "If he doesn't, then why do you keep this?"

Chantley's gut tightened. She couldn't answer his question.

He sighed. "This explains a lot. I felt like you did things that created distance between us and didn't fully accept me. It confused me, but now I see what was going on."

"It's not like that at all," she protested.

Sam pushed his glasses up his nose. "Actually, it is exactly like that." He cradled his chin with his fingers. "You see, I'm remembering something from my regression that didn't make sense. I pushed it aside then, but now I understand it perfectly. Do you recollect what I described at the gate?"

"You saw me."

"Yes. But I also saw someone else—a young man. You were helping him escape. He looked scared and guilty about something. It confused me. You were holding his hand, pulling him out. I didn't put it together at the time, but now it's obvious." He shook his head. "I don't know why I didn't see this before."

"No, it couldn't be!" She shook her head. "Even if I had a relationship with the man in that life, what relevance does it have now?"

"Are you serious? Think about everything you've told me." He flashed Vijay's photo in front of her again. "You think there's no connection with this?"

She couldn't deny the conclusion. *I did persist in comparing Sam to Vijay, which interfered with our relationship.* So this was the secret of their unhappiness! In their previous lives and in this one. Her eyes dropped. *I have been so busy examining Sam's faults that I never examined my role in the episode.* She had brought discordance and unhappiness into their relationship then, and it followed them into this life.

"This is why we kept having arguments, isn't it?" she asked. Sam nodded his head.

All the unfinished business of their previous lives resurfaced when she met Sam, and now, everything has become clear. Sam had his faults, but hers were more subtle and much deeper. What kind of relationship did she share with this long-dead unknown man? How long had it lasted? She shook her head in disbelief. She had never understood what she had been doing the past few months—what brought her to America and what secrets she had hidden. But, shockingly, now, everything was becoming clear.

She sat down. "You're right. I've been sabotaging our relationship all this time, haven't I?"

He laughed out loud. Chantley's eyes widened. Humor was the last thing she expected. Previously, such an event would have produced arguments and recriminations.

"You're not upset!" she remarked.

"Not at all," he replied. He sat next to her. "I'm glad the truth is finally out, and we understand everything. It will allow us to move on. So what's the point of being negative?" He shifted his gaze. "What's funny is that we kept looking at each other's faults when we should have been looking at our own. As they say, we're all sinners. There's no one perfect in this world."

The gloom lifted. The hurt, anger, and disappointment she felt evaporated. Gone were the infatuation and the overwhelming desire of their first encounter. She looked at Sam and noticed, for the first time, a nervousness about him. He fidgeted with his fingers. He was nothing more than a sincere young man making strides in understanding life and his place in it.

"Is that it?" he asked. "Is this goodbye?"

Chantley raised her eyebrows. Did they still have a chance? Was it something she wanted?

Sam shrugged his shoulders. "We're finally being honest with each other."

Chantley's mind was clear. The voice in her mind that constantly questioned her disappeared. "I appreciate that," she stated, "but I'm not ready to make a commitment." She looked into Sam's eyes. "I don't want to make the same mistake of rushing into something."

"Like we did before?"

"Exactly. I hurried into it because I was insecure, especially about my mother. I was rebounding from a broken heart. I became dependent on you, and mostly, I felt an overwhelming attraction."

"Same here." He rubbed his chin. "I've had some bad break-ups where there's been a lot of guilt and resentment. I don't find that here. I've never been in a platonic relationship before, but I'm glad we never got physical. It's allowed us to keep our friendship."

Chantley nodded her head. "Let's take it easy. I don't mind keeping in touch and seeing what happens. But no promises, no commitments."

Sam nodded his head in agreement. "What will you do?"

"Maybe I can teach yoga. After all, it's what I love. And I'll find a place to live. That way, I can make decisions based on security and equality, not neediness." She looked at him. "It's a more mature way of approaching things."

Sam laughed. "Reality, huh."

Chantley smiled back. "Yes. It's a wonderful thing, isn't it?" She stopped in surprise. Reality was something she would have never embraced earlier in her life.

He pushed his hat back. "I remember something you said in Boulder. That Americans need to re-establish relationships based on equality to overcome the past. You remember?"

"You told me it was a naïve suggestion."

"Now, I think it's something profound." Sam rubbed his chin reflectively. "As a black man in this country, I must settle myself. Make money and get my own place. Then, when we're secure, we can re-establish relationships."

"I need to do the same thing and stand on my own feet" she added. "And see where it takes us."

"I like where you're going," said Sam. "If it works out, great. And if it doesn't, we'll have no regrets, no bitterness."

His acceptance of her decision gave her hope. Could they come to a place where they shared a common space? She noticed something else in his demeanor. An acceptance of her as an equal, as a partner.

Chantley had an idea. Sam did his part; now, she had to perform one last act before moving into the future.

"Sam, please give me the box." He handed it to her. "Come with me."

They left the pavilion and walked down the garden. Chantley picked a handful of tiny anemones with milky white petals and dark purple stamens from the garden. She walked to the end of the jetty and, when they stopped at the water's edge, removed the lid from the box and stuffed the letters. Laying her mother and Vijay's photos on top, she placed the tiny flowers around them in a wreath and tightly closed the lid.

She knelt and placed the box into the water. It bobbed with the waves before catching the current and drifting downstream. The sun glinted off the metal, and several minutes later, its reflection joined a thousand other sparkles in the crystal waters, all heading for the boundless ocean, and watched it disappear into the distance.

About the Author

Mohan Ashtakala is an initiated Hindu Vaishnava priest who has lived in yoga ashrams across India. His goal is to expose the authentic narratives of the Yoga tradition through the medium of modern, page-turning novels. He edited and published a community newspaper in Denver, Colorado, for thirteen years.

Mohan lives in Calgary, Canada, with his wife Anuradha, son Hrishi, daughter Gopi, and Lila, the family's Boston Terrier. He can sometimes be spotted absent-mindedly chanting mantras in the city's parks.

www.mohanauthor.com.com
www.facebook.com/mohan.ashtakala

End

If you enjoyed this book, please leave a review.

www.ingramcontent.com/pod-product-compliance
Lightning Source LLC
Chambersburg PA
CBHW072108020726
47501CB00003B/767